Tessa and Weston.

THE

BEST

Christmas

EVER

ABBIE EMMONS

www.100daysofsunlight.com

www.abbieemmonsauthor.com

ISBN: 978-1-7339733-3-5

For the WritersLife Wednesday community,
with all my love

TESSA

DECEMBER 11

THERE'S NOTHING MORE MAGICAL THAN THE FIRST SNOW—
especially when it happens while you're sleeping.

I fall asleep to a subdued world of grayish brown and awaken to
a winter wonderland outside my bedroom window. Every branch of
every tree is frosted in white and sparkling in the morning sun. I smile
at the sight of it, a thrill of childish excitement lighting up in my heart.

The first thing I do is grab my phone and snap a photo of the
magical sight outside my window. I send it to Weston.

TESSA:
SNOW!!

While waiting for him to reply, I put on a sweatshirt and slide my
feet into some fuzzy socks. It's finally beginning to feel like winter.

Like Christmas.

My phone vibrates with a new message. I smile when his name
lights up on the screen.

WESTON:
I noticed

I'm about to roll my eyes at his snarky comeback, when—
THUD!
A snowball splatters against my bedroom window.
What on earth?
I stare for a moment, stunned. Then I rush to the window and peer out. Past the remnants of snow on the glass, I spot a familiar boy standing on my front lawn. A boy with an obnoxiously optimistic smile on his face. He completes the perfect winter scene, our snowy suburb shimmering around him like a Norman Rockwell painting.

I smile, throwing the window open and sticking my head out. "Weston! What are you doing here?"

"Serenading you awake!" he says, reaching one hand out theatrically. "Oh, Juliet! Juliet! Wherefore art thou, Juliet?"

I burst out laughing. "Shh! You'll wake the whole neighborhood."

"They're already awake. You're the only one still sleeping."

"Hey! I am *not* sleeping."

"You were just a minute ago."

I lift my chin. "How do you know that?"

"Because." He grins, forming another snowball in his gloved hands. "You always text me as soon as you wake up."

He knows me too well. I bite down on a smile, feeling myself blush.

"Well, you might have at least *told* me you were coming," I criticize, feeling rather lofty—I'm still leaning out my bedroom window, looking down on him.

"What fun is that?" Weston calls back. "You need more surprises in your life, Tessa."

"Oh, really?"

He nods, giving me that mischievous smile of his. "Like this!" he shouts, and throws the snowball at me.

I duck just in time. The snowball flies through my window and shatters on my bedroom floor. I gasp, popping back up to find Weston laughing on the front lawn.

Impertinent boy! I want to slap him for throwing that snowball at me. But I also want to kiss him.

A surprised laugh spills past my lips as I scream out the window, "You're going to pay for that!"

I scoop up the snow off my floor and squish it back into a ball, running downstairs as fast as my feet will carry me. The sweet smell of waffles fills the air as I fly through the kitchen, startling Grandma.

"Tessa! What on earth are you doing?"

I laugh maniacally, not stopping to explain. Instead, I run to the front door and burst out into the winter wonderland—forgetting all about shoes.

Weston's eyes widen when I come flying out the door, sprinting at him like a madwoman. I crash straight into him, throwing my arms around his neck. He laughs and staggers back a few steps.

"Well, what do you know? I got the recluse to come outside."

I look up into his sparkling gray-blue eyes, trying to catch my breath. "This is for serenading me like Romeo," I say, then reach up on my tiptoes and kiss his lips.

My heart flutters uncontrollably as a rush of dizzy warmth swirls through me, making everything else fall away. He smells so good, like fresh air and first snow and that spicy guyish scent I'm quickly becoming obsessed with. I can barely feel the cold with his arms circled around my waist, holding me gently as we kiss.

Then I remember the snowball melting in my hand.

Payback.

I can't help grinning as I ease off his lips to whisper innocently, "And this... is for throwing a snowball at me."

I shove the snow down the back of his jacket.

"AGH!"

He recoils in surprise while I start laughing. "You savage girl!" he roars, grabbing another handful of snow and winding back to throw it at me.

I dive out of the way, shrieking and laughing. "*You* started it!"

Thus, battle commences. We dart around the front yard, firing snowballs at each other and filling the air with a flurry of sparkling white. Weston has better aim and hits me far more than I hit him, which doesn't seem fair. I'd want to smack him if he weren't so cute.

Finally, Grandma steps out onto the porch to see what all the commotion is about.

"Weston!" She smiles when she sees him. "I should have known. Tessa doesn't get up that fast for anyone else. Tessa, what on earth are you doing in the snow with no shoes on? Come inside, both of you. I just made waffles."

The mention of waffles has us both racing inside the house. I'm still out of breath from our spontaneous snowball fight, my fuzzy socks are caked with snow, and my hands are freezing. I breathe into them, trying to get the feeling back in my fingertips.

"Hey, that's my job," Weston says, stepping in and enfolding my fingers in his strong, warm hands. It feels amazing after coming in out of the cold. For a moment I just stare at him, a lovestruck grin spreading over my face.

I still can't believe he's my boyfriend. Even after three months, the reality hasn't quite sunk in yet. Maybe it's because we spent the whole summer together as friends. Well, enemies at first—but when I finally let Weston into my heart, there was no getting him out.

That sunny September day when I first truly saw him was only the beginning. I didn't think it was possible to love him more than I already did, but in that moment, I fell completely head over heels. And my life has never been the same since.

I *did* stare, at first—only because I never in a million years expected him to be an amputee. I couldn't believe he'd been able to keep it a secret from me all summer. We talked for hours that day. We sat in the park, and I asked him a hundred questions, and he gave me a hundred answers. We talked until the sun set, and as the sky turned pink and orange, he asked me if I'd be his girl. I smiled and said, "I thought I already was." And he laughed.

Since that day, we've been inseparable.

He is my sunshine.

And I am his.

It's not until we're devouring waffles at the kitchen table that Weston tells me his real reason for showing up this early.

"It's Saturday," I point out, pouring maple syrup over my food. "Don't you believe in sleeping in on the weekend?"

"Nope. And all the boys are home, which means Mom is going crazy… so I said I'd take them sledding to get them out of her hair for a while. Wanna come?"

"Sledding? Me?"

"You say that like you've never been."

"Of course I've been sledding. But not in years."

"Perks of having little brothers," Weston says. "You can act like a five-year-old without being judged for it."

I roll my eyes, smiling. "Grandma, are you okay with me going sledding with Weston and his brothers?"

"I don't see why not," Grandma says from the counter, where she is ladling more waffle batter into the iron. "Just as long as you're home by four o'clock."

"What's happening at four o'clock?"

"Oh, nothing important. I just... want you to come with me to do some Christmas shopping."

By the way she says it, I can tell that's not all—I can tell she's planning some sort of surprise. I'm usually not a fan of those—however, Christmas is an exception. The holidays are all about surprises and secret delights. It's part of the magic, so I try my best to quell my curiosity and ask nothing.

I suppose I'll find out at four o'clock.

WESTON

DECEMBER 11

"LAST ONE TO THE TOP IS A ROTTEN EGG!" AIDAN SCREAMS, kicking up snow as he charges past me with his empty sled.

"Hey, that's not fair," I holler after him. "I'm pulling Noah! And he's getting too big for this." I fire a glare over my shoulder at my youngest brother, who is sprawled on his back in the sled.

"I am *not* too big for it!" he shrieks, chucking a handful of snow at me. "You're just too slow!"

"Well, I think I'm pretty fast for a guy without legs." I shoot Tessa a smile. She's wearing a pink puffer jacket and a fuzzy white hat with a pom-pom on it, and she looks more like she belongs on the streets of Manhattan, not trekking through a snow-covered golf course with a pack of wild boys.

I wish I could say that Noah is the only thing slowing me down, but he's not. My prosthetic legs are the real enemy of progress. It's awkward enough to walk through the snow with *real* legs, so you can imagine how much more difficult it is with fake ones. Thankfully, I've had enough practice to not fall on my face in front of Tessa.

But my brothers don't treat me any different because of it. They still expect me to play the reindeer.

"Aidan's gonna win!" Noah wails, throwing another snowball at my back. "Hurry up!"

"Noah," Tessa says in that sweet, mom-like voice of hers, "your brother is going to make you get out and walk in a minute."

"If we had a dog, he could pull Noah in the sled," Henry pipes up hopefully.

Tessa frowns. "A dog?"

"Henry, Mom and Dad already told you that we can't get a dog. It's too much work."

"But *I'd* be the one taking care of it," Henry insists. "Mom and Dad wouldn't have to do anything. And it wouldn't just be for me, you know. It could be a watchdog. Everyone should have a watchdog. Don't you think, Tessa?"

I grunt. "Don't drag Tessa into this."

Tessa shoots me a playful smirk. "Oh, I completely agree, Henry. Why shouldn't you have a dog? If you're really going to take care of it."

"Yeah! See, that's what I said! But Mom thinks they shed too much. She's always coming up with some problem every time I talk about it."

"Well, some dogs don't shed," Tessa points out smartly. "What kind do you want?"

"A golden retriever."

"Oh." She laughs. "Well, they *do* shed. A lot."

Henry sighs and kicks at the snow.

We finally reach the top of the hill, where Aidan is sitting on his sled, stockpiling snowballs. "What took you guys so long?" he sneers.

"Shut up!" Noah screams, jumping off my sled so suddenly I

almost face-plant in the snow.

"Ugh, Noah—Aidan, quit picking on him, alright?"

But Aidan has already launched one of his snowballs at Noah, which of course makes a fight break out between them. Noah starts throwing snowballs back at him, roaring like a baby tiger as he gets blasted in the face.

"Hey, hey, hey, guys—stop!" I jump into the line of fire. My little brothers halt their snowball fight to stare at me. "Let's settle this like gentlemen, shall we?"

Noah blinks, snow on his chin. "How?"

"Well, Aidan made it to the top of the hill first… but we all know that the *real* winner is the one who makes it to the bottom first."

"Let's go!" Aidan drops his snowball and dives into his sled.

"Hey—" I leap forward and grab the rope. "You gotta wait for Noah, or else you'll be a dirty cheater."

Aidan moans, planting his boots in the snow. "Fine. Hurry up, Noah!"

"Henry, you go with Noah."

"But I'm old enough to go by myself!" Noah whines.

I cross my arms over my chest. "Not if you're still too much of a baby to walk up the hill by yourself."

Noah pouts, but goes along. While Henry climbs into the sled with him, I grab Aidan by the collar of his jacket and say in a low voice, "If you don't let Noah win, I'll hide your Xbox somewhere you'll never find it."

He whips around, eyes wide. "You're so mean!"

"*You're* mean. Noah's the youngest. Come on. Go easy on him."

He groans. "*Fiiiiiine.*"

I turn to find Tessa watching me with a bemused smile on her face.

"Okay, Tessa, ready to show them how it's done?"

She giggles and rolls her eyes. "I told you, I haven't been sledding in years."

"That'll be my excuse when we lose." I wink at her and get on the sled. Tessa plops herself down in front of me, and I circle my arms around her waist. Sledding is definitely better with a girlfriend.

Actually, I'm beginning to realize that *everything* is better with a girlfriend.

"Okay, ready?"

"Yep!" Aidan says, already perched on the edge of the slope.

"Henry?"

He gives me a thumbs-up, and Noah bounces up and down in front of him. "Let's go!"

"Wait," I mutter, nudging my and Tessa's sled up a few feet. "On your marks... get set... go!"

We all fly off the edge of the slope in unison, sending up bursts of snow in the sunlight. Tessa screams a little, squeezing my legs and shrinking back into me, which makes me laugh. My brothers fly past us, zipping down the hill in a chaos of shouts and laughter.

"Weston, watch out for that snowbank!" Tessa shrieks.

"What snowbank?"

We crash into it.

The impact sends us both spilling out of the sled and landing on top of each other in a tangled heap. We start laughing, and Tessa rolls off me, yanking my hat down over my eyes. "You did that on purpose!"

"I thought we could just fly over it," I say, pulling my hat off to look at her. "I guess my idea didn't work."

Tessa gasps and scoops up a handful of snow. "You savage boy–"

"Don't you dare put that down my neck again!" I roll out of the way, grabbing my own handful of snow to fight back properly armed.

"No!" Tessa laughs, diving to the side—but I grab her arm and manage to shove my snow-filled hand down the back of her puffy pink jacket. It's probably not a very romantic thing to do, but I can't resist.

"How dare you!" she screams, writhing at the cold.

I stifle a laugh. "You started it."

"*You* started it when you crashed us into the snowbank!"

"Well, I didn't *mean* to—"

"Oh, I think you did." Tessa glares at me, her face all pink. Somehow, she's even cuter when she's mad at me. "I swear, Henry is more mature than you are."

I tackle her into the snow and look down into her sparkling blue eyes. "I'm sorry. Will this make up for it?"

I lean down and softly capture her lips. They taste like candy and feel like silk, and I still can't believe I get to do this. I can't believe how awesome it feels when she kisses me back, her hands sliding up my neck and making me forget what we were even doing before.

"Yes," she whispers through a breathless laugh. "That definitely makes up for it."

※ ※ ※

When we get back home, the boys are exhausted. Mom is happy to see them yawning, and even happier to see Tessa walk in the door after me. She asks her how she's been, how her grandparents have been, etcetera. She loves Tessa and gets all gooey-eyed when she sees us together.

It still feels crazy to bring a girl home with me. We've only been dating for three months, but my parents already treat Tessa like she's part of the family. She fits in so effortlessly, it makes me feel like we've always been together.

"Are you cold?" I ask her when I notice that she's shivering in her T-shirt.

She nods, rubbing her arms. "My sweater got wet. Thanks to *you* shoving snow down my coat."

I bite back a smile. "I'll give you one of mine."

She follows me upstairs to my room. Thankfully, I remembered to make my bed this morning. But that doesn't stop Tessa from wrinkling her nose and saying, "It's a mess in here."

"Yeah, okay, it's not as spotless as your model home bedroom."

Tessa laughs as I pull a gray hoodie out of a pile of clean laundry I keep forgetting to put away. Somehow, she looks beautiful in everything—even my hoodie that's way too big for her. She nuzzles her face into the collar, her eyes softening as she looks up at me.

"What's that smile for?" I say.

"Nothing, just… This is the first time you've given me one of your hoodies."

"Is that a monumental thing?"

Tessa rolls her eyes. "Yeah! It's romantic."

"How?"

She sighs and shakes her head. "You don't understand girls at all, Wes."

"No," I say with a sheepish laugh. "I don't. I've never had a girlfriend before, you know."

"Well, I've never had a boyfriend before."

"That's good."

Tessa quirks one eyebrow. "Why?"

"Because that means I'm the best boyfriend you've ever had."

She laughs and loops her arms around my neck. "You are," she whispers, her eyes darting over my face. "So far."

12

"So far?"

She giggles, leaning her forehead against my chest.

I shake my head. "Apparently I'm not the only one who doesn't know how to be romantic. Jeez…"

"I was just pulling your leg," Tessa says.

"Don't. It might come off."

That makes her laugh even harder and pop up on her tiptoes to plant a quick kiss on my lips. We head back downstairs, where Mom is making hot cocoa for the boys, who are now playing video games in the den. Noah yanks on my arm and begs me to play with them, but Mom says, "Let Weston have some time alone with Tessa." Noah shuffles off with his cocoa, whining about how I'm "old and boring" now that I have a girlfriend.

Maybe he's right. Before I met Tessa, I would never have spent a Saturday afternoon on the couch in the living room, drinking cocoa and looking through family photo albums. That's what Tessa wants to do, and I'm happy as long as she's cuddled up next to me with her head on my shoulder.

"I love photo albums," she says. "It's like stepping back in time… experiencing a moment that will never happen again." She smiles, looking up at me. "Like the Polaroids you took for me when I was blind."

"Mm, that was a good idea, wasn't it?"

"A very good idea."

"Romantic, right?"

She grins, nodding. "Very romantic."

She looks so damn cute in my hoodie, with her damp hair and rosy cheeks. Our fingers are laced together in her lap as she flips the pages of the album. It's an old one, but not too old. No embarrassing baby photos of me, thank god. Just a lot of Aidan. Henry winning a spelling bee. Me playing on the soccer team, sometime in middle school. Mom pregnant with Noah. Christmases, Thanksgivings. Awkward group photos from family reunions. Then there's a time jump to when I turned thirteen.

"Is this you and Rudy?" Tessa asks, peering at the photo.

"Yep. That was his bar mitzvah. The day I hurt myself, actually…"

"Oh, wow." Tessa goes silent for a moment, and I know what she's looking at.

My legs.

My real, flesh-and-blood legs.

But she only says, "You're both so cute," and keeps flipping.

Most people look at their old photos and see different stages of their life, every year a new age, a new grade, a new milestone.

For me, it's like all the photos are divided into just two stages of my life:

Before and After.

It's weird to look at pictures from Before. To see myself standing next to Rudy or my brothers. No different than them.

Tessa keeps turning the pages, and we transition from the Summer Before to the Winter After. There's a big gap of photos without me, and Tessa looks confused.

"How come there are no pictures of you?"

"I was in the hospital. And rehab. I didn't really feel like having my picture taken."

Tessa blushes a little, looking down. "No, I suppose not."

"Oh, here's one," I say, pointing to the top of the page. "That was my room at rehab."

Tessa tilts her head, studying the photo. It was before I got my prostheses. I'm sitting in a wheelchair, looking skinny and weak, smiling wearily for Dad, who was taking the picture. Mom stands behind my wheelchair, Henry and Aidan at my side, and Noah sits in my lap, wearing a Santa hat. We're all smiling, but none of us looks happy.

"Was it Christmas?" Tessa asks, thrown off by the Santa hat—which looks weirdly out of place in the colorless room.

"Yeah. Mom didn't want me to feel left out, so she brought the boys there, and we opened gifts together. Dad even brought this little fake tree, and Mom made us all sing carols around it. Some of the nurses even came in and joined us." I smile a little, remembering it. "My parents tried to make it good for me, but... it was the worst Christmas ever."

Tessa pushes a sad smile onto her face, getting kind of misty-eyed as she listens to the story. "I'm so sorry you had to go through all that."

"Don't be," I say, kissing her hairline. "I got exactly what I asked for a couple of weeks later."

"And what was that?"

I reach down and knock on my prosthetic leg. "These."

Tessa grunts a laugh. "You always look on the bright side, don't you?"

"Mm-hmm. You should try it sometime."

"Excuse me—I look on the bright side a lot."

"Really?"

"Yes!" She smacks my arm. "In fact, I have a very, *very* optimistic thing to say."

"Holy crap. Let's hear it."

She bites on a smile, leaning closer to my ear to whisper, "I think this will be the *best* Christmas ever."

I laugh softly, giving her hand a squeeze. "I know it will."

TESSA
DECEMBER 11

WHEN I WALK IN THE FRONT DOOR, GRANDMA DOESN'T LOOK like she's ready to go shopping. She's vacuuming the stairs, still wearing yoga pants.

"Oh! Tessa!" She straightens up when she sees me, turning off the vacuum. "You're early."

"I am?" I push up the sleeve of Weston's hoodie to glance at my watch. "It's three thirty. I didn't want to be late. Should I... go get ready?"

"You can help me with this first."

It seems odd—last-minute cleaning before going Christmas shopping. Usually, Grandma saves all the housework for Monday. But I don't ask questions; I just take the vacuum upstairs and finish the tedious chore.

I tidy my room a bit, making the bed that I only hastily threw together before I left this morning, arranging the pillows, decluttering my desk. Weston still brings me flowers every week. Red twist spray carnations this time, because it's Christmas. I smile, remembering the first time he brought me flowers—how I'd wanted to throw the jar at his head, I was so angry. But he was as stubborn as a mule. He put up with my bad moods. He loved me at my worst.

I snuggle my face into his hoodie, breathing in the spicy scent of him. I never want to take it off, but I should probably wear something slightly more fashionable for shopping. With the greatest reluctance, I change into a white turtleneck and twist my hair into a tidier bun before heading back downstairs.

"Grandma? I'm ready whenever you are."

She's in the kitchen now, putting dishes away.

I stop in the doorway, raising an eyebrow. "Are we going shopping, or... cleaning the house?"

Grandma laughs a little, nervous. "Well..."

I fold my arms over my chest. "Why do I get the feeling there's something you're not telling me? I knew you were planning some kind of surprise this morning. What is it?"

She takes a breath to explain, but before she can get a word out—

A knock comes from the front door.

Grandma's eyes light up. She glances over her shoulder at the clock, then turns back to me with a smile. "I think you should go see who's at the door."

This is so strange.

I frown, puzzled, and head down the hallway. Maybe it's FedEx, delivering some surprise Christmas gift for me. But isn't it kind of early for gifts? And how would Grandma know exactly what time a package would be delivered?

I stop guessing and instead just open the door.

And there, standing on the front porch, is the very last person I expected to see.

"Mom?"

"Hi, Tessa!" she exclaims, throwing her arms around me.

I freeze up, stunned. The scent of cigarettes and cheap perfume hits my lungs as she gives me the tightest bear hug in the world. I try to hug her back as best I can, but my mind is reeling.

"What are you doing here?" I manage to ask when I can breathe again.

But Mom doesn't hear my question. She steps back to look at me, laughing like she can't believe I'm real. "Oh, my goodness! Look at you—you're as tall as me! And your hair is so long and beautiful…"

It *has* been a year since we've seen each other, but she looks exactly the same as I remember. Blonde hair that touches her shoulders, blue eyes that nearly vanish when she smiles, '90s-thin eyebrows and smudgy makeup that she appears to have slept in. She's wearing a navy-blue NY Giants hoodie and sweatpants, which she also appears to have slept in.

"Come on in, Heather," Grandma says. "Oh, it's so good to see you!"

"Hi, Ma!" She chuckles, stamping the snow off her dirty boots and stepping inside to hug Grandma.

"How was your drive?"

"It was fine. Your usual Saturday traffic, but it wasn't too bad once I got on the highway."

I have no idea what she's doing here. Yes, she visits every year at the holidays, but she doesn't come until Christmas Day. Why is she here two weeks too soon? Why is Grandma acting like this is normal?

After a moment, Mom notices my bewildered staring and says to Grandma, "Wow, Ma, I didn't think you could keep a secret!" Another robust laugh bursts out of her.

"Of course I can," Grandma argues, with a modest smile. "Is your suitcase in the car?"

My stomach plummets.

Suitcase?

"Oh, yeah. Shit—I forgot it." Mom swats one hand dismissively in the air. "I'll have Dad get it later. Is he still out doing his churchy thing?"

Grandma replies, but I don't hear what she says. The world seems to muffle out as my mind starts spinning uncontrollably.

She's *staying?*

How long is she staying?

How could Grandma not tell me?

Is Grandpa in on this, too?

A flare of irritation rises in my chest, but I force an unruffled smile onto my face. I can't let Grandma see how annoyed I am by this little "surprise." Doesn't she know that I *hate* surprises? Didn't she learn from the whole newspaper disaster?

I guess she thought I would be happy to see my mother.

And I am.

But not with a *suitcase.*

Grandma is all smiles as she puts the kettle on, chatting with Mom about the weather and roads—as if it's a normal occurrence for her to casually drop by for tea.

When I can't stand the uncertainty any longer, I interrupt their small talk, hoping my voice doesn't sound too brusque as I come right out and say, "So, Mom, are you staying for the weekend?"

Mom turns to Grandma with a grin. "You really didn't tell her?"

I clench my jaw. All this talking-over-my-head business is starting to get on my nerves.

"No," Grandma replies, looking rather pleased with herself. "It's a complete surprise."

Mom claps her hands together, laughing like this is some sort of comedy. Then she turns to me and cheerfully declares, "I'm staying for Christmas!"

"*What?*" I sputter in disbelief. "But that's… impossible! I-I mean, how can you have that much time off work?"

Mom shrugs. "I'm sorta between jobs at the moment. Unemployed, as they call it in the real world."

She's unemployed.

She's staying for two weeks.

Oh my god.

"I thought it would be nice to spend some *real* time together this Christmas," Mom says, grasping my arms. "You know, do some mother-daughter things, catch up on life. Before you know it, you'll be off at college and too busy to hang out with your folks."

I'm not interested in going to college. And even if I was, I would never be too busy to hang out with the people I love.

She obviously doesn't know me very well.

But then, I don't know *her* very well, either. Maybe that's why it feels so intrusive that she's just shown up out of the blue like this, with plans to stay for the next *two weeks*. She feels like a stranger in my house. A stranger who wants to spend "mother-daughter" time with me.

It's all so sudden, so jarring. I feel like my world is a snow globe and someone is shaking it upside down.

But I don't let my true feelings show, for Grandma's sake alone. I don't want her thinking that I'm annoyed or upset by this "surprise" of hers.

So instead, I force a weary smile and say, "That sounds great, Mom."

❄ ❄ ❄

The rest of the night is awkward. Grandpa comes home from prayer meeting at six and does *not* seem surprised to see Mom. That's when I realize that both my grandparents were in on this secret.

I guess they *didn't* learn from the newspaper thing.

Mom yammers on about the job she doesn't have anymore and the sky-high rent she has to pay on her apartment and all the various problems with her car. I help Grandma make dinner and don't say much of anything the whole time—until we're sitting down eating, and Mom finally thinks to ask me about the accident.

"So, I can't remember—was it two months that you lost your sight for?"

I shift uncomfortably in my chair. "A little over three months."

"Wow…" She shakes her head. "That must have been tough."

I hold back a sarcastic laugh. "Yeah, it *was* tough… being completely blind."

An awkward silence settles between us.

Grandpa clears his throat. "Tessa was a real trooper for getting through it all."

"Well." I press my lips into a little smile. "I couldn't have done it without Weston."

Mom raises one skinny eyebrow. "Weston?"

"The boy who helped Tessa with her blog while she was blind," Grandma explains. "I thought for certain I mentioned him… Well, I'm sure Tessa will want to tell you all about him herself." She grins knowingly at me, which really piques Mom's interest.

"Oh yeah?" she says eagerly, turning to me. "Who is he?"

I twirl a lock of hair, feeling myself blush. "Uh… he's my boyfriend."

Mom gasps, her eyes wide. "Boyfriend?" She slaps the table. "Get out of here! You're dating him?"

I grin, nodding. It still makes my heart swell to say that. To call Weston *my boyfriend.*

"Ohhh, that got her to smile!" Mom laughs, which makes everyone laugh, which makes me blush hotter. "Well, I won't make you talk about it in front of Grandpa, but I want to hear *all* about him later." She winks pointedly at me, and for the first time tonight, I find it not so hard to smile.

Weston is the one conversation I'm happy to have with anyone.

When dinner is finished, Grandma says she can clean up the kitchen. "Why don't you go show your mom her room? Grandpa already took her suitcase up."

"Okay," I say, and escort Mom upstairs, which takes a while because she keeps stopping every two steps to point out a picture on the wall, or peek her head inside random doors to see where they go. She looks into my room and says it's beautiful, "just like on HGTV." Two doors down the hall is the guest room, where we find Mom's pink suitcase parked at the end of the bed.

Just seeing it makes my heart sink a little—a final confirmation that I wasn't just dreaming.

She's staying.

Until Christmas.

"So," she says, sitting cross-legged on the bed. "Now that it's just us girls... tell me all about this boyfriend of yours." She pats the mattress.

I laugh under my breath and sit down beside her. Starting at the very beginning, I tell her the story of how I met Weston, and all the sweet things he did for me when I was blind. The flowers. The Polaroids. The walks to town. The day at the amusement park.

"So you fell in love with him before you even saw him?" Mom asks.

"Yeah. I did. Then he told me that he was in love with *me*, and…" I hesitate, arriving at the complicated part of the story. That messy week of confusion and unanswered calls and secrets and lies…

I skip over all of that to the good part.

"Well, eventually, after I got my sight back, we met each other face-to-face. And I saw him for the first time."

"And did he look like how you imagined?"

I smile and nod. "Even better than I imagined."

Mom squeals, clasping her hands together. "Oh, I want to see a picture!"

I pull my phone out of my pocket; there's a selfie of us right on my lock screen. I flip it around for Mom to see.

"Oh, my word—stop it! You two are so cute… And he is a *doll*."

"Right?" I giggle, my heart glowing like the sun. I never get tired of that picture. His is the first face I see in the morning and the last face I see at night.

"I'm so happy for you," Mom says, rubbing my shoulder. "See, sometimes a good thing can come out of a bad thing. If you'd never gotten into that accident, you might never have met Weston."

"That's true."

Mom goes quiet for a moment, and when her voice returns, it's more subdued. "You know… when you and Ma got into that accident, it made me really think. What if I had lost one of you? Or both of you?" She shakes her head, like she doesn't even want to contemplate that. "It was a miracle you lived, Tessa. And that got me thinking… life is short. I guess I just wanted to come see you and spend some time together. I would have come sooner, but… I was waiting for the right

23

moment. I knew you were going through a lot over the summer, dealing with your... blindness and all. I didn't want to add to the stress. Grandma was the one who suggested I come earlier for Christmas. And since I'm out of work right now... 'Tis the season for spending time with your family, right?"

I push a feeble smile onto my lips. "You're right. It is." I feel like I ought to say more than that, but I don't have the heart to lie and tell her that I want to spend time with her.

The fact is, I don't.

I'm fine with her visiting every year on Christmas Day. I survive the awkwardness because it's just one day, one dinner, one gathering. But two weeks of mother-daughter time? When we've *never* had mother-daughter time in the past? Nothing was stopping her from visiting more often *before.* Why didn't she?

Did it literally take me almost dying in a car accident to scare her into visiting? Apparently, it made her feel guilty enough to drive all the way up here and crash my Christmas plans. Or maybe it was just convenient, since she's currently unemployed.

What makes her think she can just show up and start bonding with me now? What makes her think I'll *want* to?

The whole thing rumples my mind. I'm too tired to think about it any longer—too tired to fake one more smile. All I want to do is go to bed and call Weston.

But by the time I shower and change into my pajamas, Weston has already sent me his goodnight text.

WESTON:
Dude I'm wiped gotta sleeeeep
goodnight beautiful
love you

It was sent an hour ago, which means he's fast asleep by now. Weston is one of these "early to bed, early to rise" types. Which is healthy, I suppose—but not very helpful for my emotional stability.

I content myself by snuggling under the covers and reliving the best parts of my day. The sledding escapade with Weston and his brothers. Kissing him in the snow. Cuddling with him on the couch; looking through old photo albums together.

That's when I realize something: I forgot to tell Mom about Weston's legs.

I'd skipped over so many details in the story, the parts that would take too long to explain. Should I tell her before she meets him? I don't know how I would bring it up. It seems weird to just randomly add, "Oh, and by the way, my boyfriend is a double amputee." I would feel so superficial saying it like that. As if it matters, as if it's some defining part of him.

It doesn't define him.

It's just something that happened to him—a challenge he faced and had to overcome. Like my blindness. Nobody would introduce me by saying, "This is Tessa. She was in a car accident and was blind for one hundred days." That's past. It's over and done, and it doesn't change who I am right now. And Weston's disability doesn't change who he is, either.

So I decide to say nothing to Mom about it. If Weston wants to tell her when he meets her, that's his choice.

The stars told me

they're jealous of you

They wish they could shine

half as bright

WESTON
DECEMBER 12

TESSA:
Good morning <3
I can't wait to talk to you

> **WESTON:**
> Want to facetime?

TESSA:
I'm in church
But I'll want to later
When I get home

> **WESTON:**
> Ok
> Something wrong?

TESSA:

No not really

It's just

WESTON:

?

TESSA:

I'll tell you later

Sunday dawns warm—fifty degrees and sunny. Almost all the snow is melted by mid-morning, leaving the sidewalks in perfect condition for my blades. December can never decide if it wants to be winter or not. But that's cool by me—I've missed running through the neighborhood.

Mom tries to stop me as I'm heading out the door. "And where do you think you're going dressed like that?"

I frown. "Like what?" I look down at myself. Basketball shorts, hoodie. By the way Mom is looking at me, you would think I'm naked.

"It's freezing!"

"Mom, it's T-shirt weather out there."

She crosses her arms stubbornly. "Well, you just have to make sure you don't get too cold. You don't want the phantom pain acting up—"

"Yeah, I know. I won't take my hoodie off, okay? As much as I might want the world to admire my abs." I wink at her over my shoulder. "Bye!"

I put on my headphones and blast some heavy metal as I take off running down the street. Okay, maybe it's not exactly T-shirt weather, but the sun feels good. It's pretty amazing what a difference a change in prostheses can make. I'm slow and clumsy in the snow with my everyday legs—but on clear pavement with my running blades? I can fly.

Sure, it draws attention sometimes. But I've gotten used to the occasional thumbs-up or word of encouragement from a random stranger. It's actually kind of nice—and something that most runners miss out on.

I don't take my usual route around the block. Instead, I head toward Tessa's house. She texted me earlier when she was at church, and I could tell something wasn't right. She wanted to call me after, but I'd rather talk face-to-face.

By the time I reach West Elm Street, it's after twelve, and her grandparents' car is parked in the driveway. There's another car, too. A dirty Subaru with Pennsylvania plates.

Weird.

I pull my headphones off, letting them fall around my neck as I knock on the front door.

A minute later, it swings open, and there stands Tessa, still wearing her pretty church clothes. Curly hair, wide eyes.

"Weston! What are you doing here?"

"You said you wanted to talk. I was out running, so I thought I'd just stop by and see you. Can I come in?"

"NO—uh, I mean… Now's not a good time." She gives me a once-over, and her gaze freezes on my blades. She's seen me in them a hundred times, but now she's staring at me the way someone would if you showed up to their fancy event wearing the wrong clothes. It's kind of a weird expression; I can't make sense of it.

"Why not?" I say. "You wrapping my Christmas presents?"

Tessa laughs wearily, rubbing her forehead. "No, I…" She sighs and lowers her voice. "My mother's here."

"Your mother?"

She nods.

"The one from Pittsburgh?"

Tessa rolls her eyes. "Of course, Wes! How many mothers do I have?"

I grin, about to make a joke about that—but then I notice how genuinely annoyed she looks. "You don't seem too happy about it."

"I'm not. She wasn't supposed to be here till Christmas Day."

"Wait—so she's staying with you?"

Tessa nods gravely. "For *two weeks*."

I can tell by the look in her eyes: she's *really* not happy about it. I've learned to read those eyes, even back in the days when they couldn't see me. Now I'm an expert—one glance and I see a few layers to this: frustration, stress, too many things happening at once, messing up her plans. And beyond all that, some kind of deeper drama.

I don't ask her about any of it. Instead, I try to keep things chill and uncomplicated. "Did you tell her about your devilishly good-looking boyfriend?"

Tessa laughs a little. "Yes, of course. She's looking forward to meeting you."

"Well, here I am."

Tessa freezes. "Yeah, but—"

"No time like the present," I say, stepping around her and into the house.

She looks as if she wants to stop me, but can't find the words. She's such a fanatic about planning stuff like this, I think it blows her mind when I just act on an impulse. It's foreign to her. And it's kind of hilarious to watch her reaction.

I hear voices coming from the kitchen—Mrs. Dickinson and another woman with a rough smoker's voice. Tessa's mom. I see her the second I step through the doorway. Blonde, shortish, standing with her back to me.

Tessa's grandmother sees me immediately and smiles. "Oh—hi, Weston."

"Hey, Mrs. Dickinson."

Tessa appears at my side, putting her arm through mine just as her mother turns around to look at me.

"Mom," Tessa says, a hesitant strain to her voice, "this is Weston."

I give her one of my irresistible smiles and say, "Pleasure to meet you, ma'am."

She's about to say something in reply, but that's when her gaze falls to my legs and freezes there. Okay, so I was expecting that. Everyone goes through the Reaction: first, they stare for at least a second or two; then they quickly smile and look back up at my face, pretending they didn't see what they just saw, because they have no idea what to say about it, or if they should say anything at all.

But Tessa's mom has a different reaction. First, her eyes widen; then her mouth drops open. The look on her face could only be described as extreme shock.

That's when I realize: Tessa didn't tell her.

Well, this is awkward.

I try to think of something funny to say, but Tessa's mom beats me to it.

"Holy crap!" she blurts out. "You don't see that every day!"

I make myself laugh, because I don't know what else to do.

Tessa stiffens beside me, her face going bright red. "Mom!"

I want to say something to break the ice and let Tessa know I'm not offended, but I draw a total blank. Her mom is looking at me the way you'd stare at some crazy photoshopped clickbait on the internet, trying to decide whether or not it's real.

After a second, she snaps out of her stunned daze and laughs uneasily. "I'm sorry. I have a big mouth. I just... didn't see that coming! Tessa never said a word about you being—well, you know. About that." She gestures bluntly at my running blades. "How do you walk on those things, anyway?"

I laugh under my breath, rubbing the back of my neck. "It's easier than it looks, actually. These ones are just for running."

"Oh yeah—I've seen those guys wear them in the handicap Olympics. You know, the runners?"

I nod. "Yeah, in the Paralympics. Exactly."

"Wow..." She shakes her head in disbelief. "That's amazing! So were you born without legs, or did you—"

"Mom," Tessa cuts in, her voice as sharp as a knife, "maybe Weston doesn't want to talk about this right now." She gives her mother a scathing look, like *shut the hell up.*

I slide my hand into Tessa's and give it a little squeeze. "It's okay," I say, mostly to Tessa—but it doesn't make a difference. She looks mortified, her face is bright pink, and her eyes are on fire with indignation.

"Oops," her mom says with a chuckle. "There goes my big mouth again! It's really good to meet you, hon." She reaches out for a handshake, and it seems kind of awkwardly delayed at this point, but I go through the motions anyway.

"Good to meet you too, Mrs...?"

"Oh, just call me Heather."

That's when Tessa's grandmother cuts in with a question about how my family is doing, and we get off on some small talk that isn't about my legs. Tessa stands beside me, wordless the whole time, her body rigid, her hand sweaty and cold.

This is no good. We need to talk. Alone.

So, after a minute I say, "Well, I should be heading back," and politely make my escape. Tessa follows me out onto the front porch and lets out a big sigh when the door shuts behind us.

"Oh my god... I'm so sorry."

I give her a reassuring smile. "It's okay. I'm used to it."

But she's not. In her eyes, I can see that she's still back there in the kitchen with her mom. That horrified look is frozen on her face.

"How could she say that?" she whispers, stunned. "Did she even hear herself?"

I grunt a laugh. "Welcome to the world of having parents. They say embarrassing stuff in front of your friends. They can't help it."

Tessa looks down, like she can't meet my eyes.

I gently nudge her with my shoulder. "Hey. It wasn't that bad."

"It was awful. *She* was awful."

"Well, it looks like it bothered you much more than it bothered me."

"It *does* bother me!" Her gaze shoots up to mine for a second; there are a thousand words in her eyes. But she doesn't say any of them. Instead, she buries her face in her hands. "Ugh, I'm so embarrassed..."

My heart sinks a little, a sense of dread tightening in the pit of my stomach. I tell myself it's nothing: Tessa is just annoyed by what her mom said back there. But this is way more than just *annoyance*. I can see it, plain as day.

Shame.

"Well," I say in a soft voice, "you could have told her about it ahead of time."

Tessa lifts her face out of her hands, looking up into my eyes. "I shouldn't have to. Like, is it such a big part of who you are? I didn't think it mattered that much."

I shake my head. "It doesn't."

Tessa looks away, her face still scrunched in anguish and flushed red. I feel useless and a little confused as I think about what she just said.

I shouldn't have to.

So she didn't forget to tell her mom.

She *chose* not to tell her.

She avoided talking about it.

Why?

It would have been the easiest thing in the world to mention. Her mom still might have stared a little and asked me about the blades, but it wouldn't have been nearly as awful as Tessa apparently thinks it was.

So why didn't she just explain ahead of time?

Then it hits me. I think I know why—and it's something that Tessa would never say to my face.

The suspicion makes my stomach drop. A pang of guilt stabs through me, and I suddenly feel sick with regret. It's like a shadow that swallows me up, a ghost from my past.

"I'm sorry," I murmur. "I shouldn't have just... shown up like this."

Tessa shakes her head. "It's not your fault—it's my mom. You know I never mind your spontaneous visits."

But that's not what I meant when I said "like this."

I meant *dressed* like this.

In my running blades like this.

Why did I have to go inside and see Tessa's mom, anyway? Tessa tried to tell me it wasn't a good time. She tried to keep me outside.

Tried to keep me from embarrassing her.

The more I think about it, the sicker I feel.

"I should go."

Tessa doesn't reply. She just looks down at her hands clasped on the railing.

I kiss the top of her head and leave.

Later that afternoon, I'm walking through the living room, and I notice the photo albums still out on the coffee table from yesterday. One is lying open, and I find myself stopping to look at the page.

It's a Before picture. Me and my brothers at Coney Island. We're all grinning into the sun, and Noah is sitting on my shoulders, his hands covering my eyes, making me laugh.

I wonder how different today would have been if I looked more like the Weston in this picture.

There wouldn't have been any awkward staring or fumbling for words. Tessa's mom would have looked at my face, not my feet. She would have asked me what grade I'm in, not how I can "walk on those things."

And most importantly, Tessa wouldn't have been embarrassed.

She said it wasn't me, it was her mom.

But I know that's not true.

I saw her face.

TESSA

DECEMBER 12

I WISH THE EARTH WOULD SWALLOW ME UP.

That's all I think as I stand on the porch and watch Weston vanish down the street. I couldn't even look him in the eyes, I was so ashamed. So mortified by my mother's behavior. I *knew* this was going to happen. When I first opened the door and saw Weston standing there in his running blades, I regretted not telling my mom all about it last night.

I had hoped that it wouldn't have been so obvious upon their first meeting—that he would have time to explain in his own way whenever he felt like it. I had hoped—irrationally, perhaps—that Mom would be polite and sensitive about Weston's disability.

But instead, she was rude and uncouth. She stared at Weston like he was some freak of nature, and she asked him the most impertinent questions. I wanted to scream at her—but I was too busy dying of embarrassment.

Weston assured me that he didn't mind, that he was used to it— but I could tell it bothered him. He seemed so crestfallen when he left.

So quiet and subdued, so *not* like my Weston. And I know it is all my fault.

Even after he's gone and I am left standing on the porch alone, his words burn in my mind.

"You could have told her about it ahead of time."

I could have. I *should* have. Oh, why didn't I? I'm so foolish, so inconsiderate! Poor Weston has to endure enough without extra insolence from my mother. I feel so guilty, having put him through that.

I go back inside to find Mom and Grandma still in the kitchen, talking in low voices. I stop in the doorway, crossing my arms firmly over my chest.

"Mom, how could you treat Weston like that?"

She turns to stare at me, eyebrows raised cluelessly. "What?"

"The way you stared at him! And the things you asked him... Could you even hear yourself?"

Mom looks shocked by my anger, which I suppose only proves her ignorance. "I didn't mean to be offensive—"

"Well, you *were* offensive. And luckily, he's used to people being rude to him, so he wasn't offended. But I am." I shake my head slowly. "I'm ashamed of you."

"Tessa." Grandma's voice is razor-sharp.

But Mom puts her hand up dismissively. "It's okay, Ma." She steps closer to me, softening her voice. "Honey, I'm sorry. I didn't mean to be rude to your boyfriend. But you should've given me some kinda warning if you didn't want me to stare."

I scoff, disgusted by her words. "Warning?" My voice wobbles, tears burning in my eyes. "Weston is the sweetest, most wonderful person you will ever meet. He shouldn't have to come with a 'warning'!"

I turn away sharply and run for the stairs. I hear Mom call after me, "I didn't mean it like that!" but I don't stop. I storm up the stairs and into my room, slamming the door shut behind me and locking it.

I throw myself onto my bed, all this anger and turmoil suddenly bursting out of me in the form of tears. I bury my face in the pillows and cry, my heart breaking for Weston.

I'm not just angry at my mother—or all the people like her. I'm angry at myself for being so thoughtless.

❄ ❄ ❄

A soft knock sounds on my bedroom door, accompanied by Grandma's voice. "Tessa? Can I come in?"

I feel stiff and cold after lying on my bed in the fetal position for an hour. My eyes are sore and weary from crying, but I haven't had the motivation to get up.

Until Grandma jiggles my doorknob.

"Tessa, please let me in."

I unfold myself, stumble to my feet and unlock the door—then immediately return to my bed before Grandma can step inside the room. I sit cross-legged, hugging a fuzzy pillow to my stomach.

"Oh, sweetheart, don't cry," Grandma says gently, sitting beside me and tucking a strand of hair behind my ear. "And don't be angry at your mom. She wasn't trying to be rude."

"She doesn't have to try," I quip darkly. "It just comes naturally to her."

Grandma gives me a disapproving look.

I sigh, pressing my fingertips to my forehead. "Why did you have to invite her, anyway?"

"Because she wanted to come and spend some time with you," Grandma says, rubbing my back. "And I thought it would be nice for us to do some catching up."

"But why now? If she really wanted to spend time with me, she would have been doing it all along."

Grandma goes quiet for a long moment. Then she says, "Your mom has made some mistakes with her life. But it's never too late to start over. She'll always be my daughter, no matter what. And you'll always be hers."

A twinge of shame spurs me in the heart. It is not guilt for the way I shouted at Mom downstairs, nor even regret for my secret thoughts and irritation last night. It is a deeper ache, hiding beneath the surface.

"Everyone deserves a second chance, Tessa. I'm not saying you have to spend *all* your time with her. But try to get along. Try to let her make it up to you." Grandma squeezes my hand. "Will you do that? For me?"

I nod stiffly. "I'll try. For you."

"Thank you." She kisses the side of my head as she stands. "I'm making some tea. Why don't you change into something comfy and come downstairs."

"Alright. I'll be down in a minute."

Grandma leaves the room, and for a long moment I just sit on my bed, staring at the wall. Thinking about the promise I made her.

To get along with Mom.

Even when she's insensitive to my sweet Weston. Even when she talks too much about herself and complains about everything else. Even when I want to scream at her.

I have to get along. For Grandma and Grandpa's sake.

These will be two long, awkward, torturous weeks... but I suppose I'll survive. I'll fulfill my duty by spending *some* time with her.

But there's only one way to salvage this Christmas: Avoid her as much as possible.

I'll make lots of plans that can't be changed. I'll hang out with Weston and his family whenever I get the chance. I'll surprise him by thinking up things for us to do together—things that will keep me out all day.

Perhaps it's unfeeling to scheme like this just to avoid being with my mom.

After all, Grandma is right.

I'll always be her daughter.

She'll always be my mother.

But what kind of mother doesn't show up when her daughter suffers a traumatic accident? What kind of mother doesn't want to be a part of her daughter's life? She may be here *now,* but she was never here when I was growing up.

I know all the talking points that justify my mom's absence: she was young, she wasn't ready to be a mother, she would have had to toss me around to different babysitters, and why do that when you have some convenient long-suffering parents standing by, ready to pick up the pieces of your falling-apart life?

I've tried to see it from her point of view—I have. I've tried to imagine what it would be like to find myself pregnant at eighteen and all alone. I would be terrified, ashamed, lost at sea. And if I had good parents like Grandma and Grandpa, I would absolutely trust them with my baby.

But I would never leave.

I would never move away and act like it never happened.

I would never make my daughter feel like a mistake that I wish I'd never made.

Warrior boy,

I will never understand

how you walked through hell

and came out with scars

but no burns

WESTON

DECEMBER 12

I THROW A STRAIGHT RIGHT AS HARD AS I CAN—THEN A LEFT uppercut, right hook, left hook. My knuckles sting against the heavy bag. Blisters coming. Don't care.

"Someone's angry."

I fire a glance over my left shoulder at Rudy, who's working combos on the next bag.

"I'm not angry," I growl angrily, wiping the sweat off my forehead.

Rudy raises his eyebrows. "Just as long as you take it out on the bag and not me."

I turn back to the heavy bag, blasting it with another combination. Jab, straight right, left hook. Driving my knee up to finish.

Gladiator Fitness has the look—and smell—of a classic boxing gym. Think rows and rows of bags of various shapes and sizes, two enclosed rings, plus all the usual equipment you find in a gym: treadmills, elliptical, cable machines, and weight racks. In other words, you feel like Rocky the minute you walk through the door.

I'm the one who dragged Rudy out to train with me on a Sunday night. He complained about it, saying we should do something "actually fun," but I couldn't think of a better way to spend the weekend than kicking Kaufmann's ass to the soundtrack of '80s rock anthems.

Okay, fine. Maybe there's another reason I feel like punching something tonight.

"You wanna spill your guts?" Rudy says after a few minutes of watching me brutalize the heavy bag like a maniac.

It's so annoying having a best friend who can see right through you.

I stop for a second to catch my breath, leaning my forearms against the bag and glancing over at him. "I don't know," I mutter. "Not really."

"Is it about Tessa?"

"Yeah…"

"Did you have a fight?"

"No." I blow out a sigh, dragging a sweaty hand over my sweaty face. "I met her mom."

"Her mom?" Rudy frowns. "But I thought she didn't live around here."

"She's visiting. For Christmas, I guess. Anyway, I was out running this morning, so I stopped by Tessa's house, and that's when I met her mom. And it turns out Tessa didn't tell her about my legs."

"Oh," Rudy says with a dry laugh. "Awkward."

"Yeah." I throw easy jabs at the bag to distract myself. "So, of course the first thing she noticed was my blades. And of course she was staring… said something kinda dumb about it. She probably didn't mean for it to sound as bad as it did. But I didn't really care, you know? I'm used to people saying stuff."

Rudy gives me a dubious look. "Well, for a guy who wasn't bothered... you sure look bothered."

I sigh. "It wasn't her mom that bothered me. It was... the way Tessa acted about the whole thing. I'd never seen her so embarrassed."

"'Course she was embarrassed. Her mom said something dumb right in front of you."

"Well, the whole thing could have been avoided if Tessa had just told her mom about my legs before she met me."

"She probably forgot."

I shake my head, a twinge of that sick feeling coming back. "She didn't forget. She told me that she didn't mention it on purpose. Because she shouldn't have to or something. That it's not important, it's not who I am."

"Well, she's right," Rudy says. "It's not."

"No, but it is *part* of me. Can't deny it. Can't hide it. And I don't want to, but..." I swallow, looking down at my bruised knuckles. "But she did. And now I can't stop thinking... Does she wish that things were different? Would she like me better if I wasn't...?"

An amputee.

I lower my voice, starting over a different way. "Was she, like... *ashamed* to tell her mom about me?"

Rudy sees me slipping. "Bro, I think you're reading too much into this."

"Am I?" I frown, not convinced. "You didn't see her face, Rudy. She looked like she wanted to melt through the floor. I know she felt bad for me, but..." I mutter a humorless laugh. "I felt bad for *her.*"

When I close my eyes, all I can see is her standing on the porch with her face in her hands. And all I feel is guilt.

"Why?" Rudy says, his voice like steel.

I just stare at him, a lump in my throat. I can't answer.

"Because you think she deserves better?"

That probably wouldn't hurt like a knife in the gut if it weren't true.

When I don't answer right away, Rudy gets pissed.

"You better say no, or I'm gonna take you into that ring and beat some sense into you—"

"No. I don't know. I just…" I shut my eyes, taking a deep breath. "Look. I don't… think about myself that way anymore. Okay? But those thoughts, they don't just… go away overnight. I still struggle with them. It's a fight."

Rudy goes quiet for a minute, thinking about it.

"Most of the time, I've got the upper hand," I say, throwing light punches at the heavy bag. "And sometimes I get cocky, thinking the fight's over and I've won. Then something like this morning happens, and… knocks me on my ass again."

Rudy nods slowly, then claps a hand on my shoulder and says, "I get it, man. I do. But you gotta keep fighting. Even when it seems like you're losing. Especially then. You taught *me* that, remember?"

I manage a tired smile. "Yeah. I remember."

"Don't forget," he says. "You've gotta teach those thoughts a lesson."

I laugh. "Should I practice on you?" I swing my thumb in the direction of the ring, which is waiting under the spotlights for a good sparring match.

Rudy grins. "Just as long as you keep that nasty uppercut to yourself."

That night as I'm getting ready for bed, Tessa video calls me. I pick up my phone, and her face fills the screen—she's in bed, wearing my hoodie, looking all sleepy and cute.

"I called a hundred times. Where were you?"

"Sorry," I grunt, sprawling out on my bed. "I was in the shower. It takes me forever."

"Oh. I thought maybe you were ignoring me."

I frown. "What? Why would I be ignoring you?"

Tessa sucks on her lower lip. "Well… because of this morning. The whole thing with my mom. I'm so sorry about all of that."

"Tessa, don't be sorry. It wasn't your fault."

"I know, but… I feel bad." She sighs, twirling a strand of hair. "I should've told her about your legs before. I just… didn't look at it from your perspective. I mean, if it was the other way around, I would've wanted you to tell *your* mom. Not that your mom would have been so rude as to stare like that. And to say those things—"

"I can't even remember what she said. Okay? That's how much I don't give a shit."

"How can you not give a—" Tessa stops herself and rephrases. "How can you not care?"

I grin, because I love watching her avoid cuss words. "I don't *care*… because it happens all the time. You've gotta get used to it if you're going to be my girlfriend."

Tessa thinks about that for a moment, a silent conflict in her eyes.

"*Can* you get used to it?" I ask quietly, hoping I don't sound as unsure as I feel.

"I don't know," Tessa murmurs. "I shouldn't have to. *You* shouldn't have to. It's not fair."

"Life's not fair."

"I know, but you've already been through so much. Only to have to put up with insolence from strangers. It makes me so angry."

I shrug. "I had to put up with *your* insolence."

Tessa's jaw drops; she stares at me, stunned. "That was different! I couldn't see you; I didn't know what I was saying. I wasn't being intentionally rude."

"Well, neither was your mom," I argue. "Most people aren't intentionally rude. They just... don't think before they speak. But I do the same thing, so how can I judge?"

Tessa squints at me through the screen, like it's a painful struggle to see it from this perspective. Then she lets out a surprised laugh.

"What?"

She shakes her head. "Nothing, just... I admire you so much."

I push a weak smile onto my face. "Well, I would hope so."

But I'm not sure *how* she admires me.

The way most strangers do, congratulating me for getting out of bed every morning and doing the ordinary things that ordinary people do? I don't want that kind of admiration—especially not from Tessa.

But I don't ask her to be more specific. Not because I'm afraid of the answer, but because I won't be able to tell if it's true.

"So, are we good?" Tessa asks, genuine worry in her eyes.

"Yes. We're good."

"Are you sure?"

"Tessa, stop. You overthink everything."

She groans, sinking back into her pillows. "You know how I am..."

"Mm-hmm. Obsessive. Controlling. Stubborn as all hell."

She scoffs. "*You're* stubborn."

"Impossible."

"Irresponsible."

I glare at her through the screen. "Smart-mouth."

"Potty-mouth."

I burst out laughing at that one. "Okay, fine. You're better than me."

"Well, I don't know about *that*," Tessa says, tipping her phone against the pillow so that it almost feels like I'm lying beside her. "We all have faults."

"True. But I think you have less than everybody else."

She smiles, shutting her eyes.

"You look tired. You should go to sleep."

"Yeah," she murmurs. "But I want to talk to you."

"We can talk tomorrow."

"Okay…"

"Hey. Don't fall asleep before you hang up. Or I'll have to listen to you snore."

She opens her eyes to glare at me. "I don't snore."

I grin. "How do you know?"

She rolls her eyes. "Goodnight, Wes."

"Goodnight, Tes."

She gives me an air-kiss.

I give her one back.

Then she hangs up.

I drop my phone on my chest, and for a long time I just lie on my bed, staring at the ceiling.

Tessa probably thinks I was flattering her, but I was dead serious. She *does* have fewer faults than anyone I've ever met. In fact, she's pretty damn close to perfect. If she put herself out there more, she'd probably have guys waiting in line to go out with her.

I joked about being the best boyfriend she's ever had because I'm the *only* boyfriend she's ever had—but now, that thought is beginning to strike me as less ironic and more intimidating.

What if she *can't* get used to the Reaction?

What if she gets tired of my disability always being a point of discussion?

What if, one day, she stops loving me because of it?

I've never doubted her before, because she never gave me a reason to. She's always treated me just like everyone else. It's easy to be around her, to be myself. She doesn't care about my legs—barely mentions them, barely even notices if I take off my prostheses when we're hanging out. I've never had cause to think that my disability made her uncomfortable.

Until today.

I wish I didn't feel like this, but there's no denying the gnawing sense of dread in the pit of my stomach. The sudden, startling fear of losing Tessa—the best part of my life.

No. I'm not going to lose her.

I'll be the best boyfriend she's ever had.

The best boyfriend she'll *ever have*.

I'll show her that we can have a perfectly normal relationship, just like other couples. Nothing awkward or different.

I'll prove to her how much I love her.

And I'll start by making this her best Christmas ever.

TESSA

DECEMBER 14

ON TUESDAY, WESTON INVITES ME TO GO WITH HIS FAMILY
to get their Christmas tree. At first, I think he means go to the
Mercantile—our historical little country store—and pick out a pre-cut
tree. That's what Grandpa and Grandma have always done.

But Weston scoffs at this idea. "You're telling me you've never
gone out in the woods and cut down your own Christmas tree?"

I laugh through the phone. "No."

"Okay, you're *definitely* coming with us, then. Unless you have
plans with your mom."

"Are you kidding? I would *much* rather hang out with you. That
is, if your parents don't mind. Are you sure there's enough room for
me?"

There is. Just barely. Weston's mom has an SUV, so he and I sit
in the way-way back; the three younger boys are seated in front of us,
occasionally peeking over their shoulders as if trying to catch us in the
act of something scandalous. But we're only holding hands and
sneaking little smiles at each other. Old Christmas classics play softly

on the radio as we drive through the wintery landscape. Weston traces "I love you" in the fog on the window. I kiss his cheek.

At last, we arrive at the tree farm. It's a quiet, tucked-away pocket of the countryside with only one house in sight: a log cabin frosted in snow, with golden lamplight glowing in the windows and a wisp of smoke climbing up from a stone chimney. The whole scene looks like a Thomas Kinkade painting.

Mr. Ludovico parks the car, and we all pile out. Aidan and Noah immediately sprint off towards the woods, which makes their mother holler after them to come back here and put their gloves on.

Weston helps by wrangling Noah and shimmying his little hands into a pair of snow gloves. "You wanna help pick out the tree?" he asks his little brother.

Noah nods fiercely.

"Well, then you gotta stay close to Mom. 'Cause you know she's the ultimate judge."

"But—Aidan's gonna go in the woods without me!"

Weston crouches down in front of Noah and says in a low voice, "If he *does* go in the woods, he's gonna get his butt smacked. You want your butt smacked?"

Noah shakes his head.

"Didn't think so." He musses Noah's beanie as he straightens up. "Now go influence the judge."

"Okay…" Noah tromps off to his mother's side.

I smile, because there is nothing cuter than the way Weston interacts with his brothers.

"Yo! Aidan!" he calls after the prodigal son, who is now about twenty yards ahead of us.

"Yeah, what is it?"

"Rock Paper Scissors for who gets to carry the ax!"

That's all it takes for Aidan to come running back to the car. "Dad said I could carry the ax! He told me before, right, Dad?"

But his dad can't hear because he's rifling around the backseat, presumably looking for the ax.

"Hey." Weston pokes Aidan in the chest. "Fight me like a man."

Aidan heaves a sigh, as if he is far too old for games like this, but Weston makes him do Rock Paper Scissors anyway. Aidan's rock aggressively smashes Weston's scissors.

"I WIN!" he yells, diving for the ax, which Mr. Ludovico has just pulled out of the car.

"Careful," his father warns. "No running with that."

"Yeah, I know…"

I frown at Mr. Ludovico. "Do you really cut the tree down with an ax?"

He grins and says, "Nope," holding up a bow saw that Aidan evidently didn't see.

I laugh, linking arms with Weston as we all head into the tree farm. The jubilant shouts of the younger boys mingle in the air with the gently falling snow, making everything feel more nostalgic. Henry lags behind his parents, looking lonely and dog-less. Weston and I lag farther still behind everyone, because we're *that* couple.

I smile and tip my head back to look up at him. "You're so good with your brothers."

Weston laughs under his breath. "It's not always easy."

"But they respect you. And you always make them get along, somehow. You'd make a good dad."

He shoots me a startled look. "Slow your roll. I'm seventeen."

"I know. I just meant, like… in the future."

Weston grins at me, a teasing sparkle in his eyes. "The future, huh?"

I blush, looking down at our hands laced together. "Yeah, you know... *future* future."

"Mm. Tell me more about this *future* future. It sounds kinda hot."

I try to give him a sharp look, but my smile gives me away. "I'm going to smack you in a minute."

"Wow." He winks at me. "It must be *really* hot."

I shove him, and he shoves me back. I threaten to put more snow down his coat, but he just laughs, wrapping his arm around my shoulders and kissing the top of my head.

"For what it's worth," he says, in a soft, husky voice, "I think you'll make a good mom. In the *future* future."

I bite on a smile, butterflies going crazy in my stomach. It makes me dizzy with happiness to think that I have a whole future to live with Weston. I want to savor every kiss, every heartbeat, every moment.

At last, the boys pick out a tree, and Noah declares it is "definitely the one." No sooner than Mrs. Ludovico agrees, Aidan is diving under the tree, hacking at it with the ax. His parents allow this for a minute, as a rite of passage. Then Mr. Ludovico steps in and says, "Alright, let your brother have a turn," and offers Weston the saw. "Want to give it a go?"

"Oh. Yeah, sure." Weston takes the saw, flashing an arrogant little grin over his shoulder at me. His parents exchange an amused look as he approaches the tree, brandishing the saw like a (rather adorable) lumberjack.

We all stand back and watch as Weston crawls under the tree and begins sawing at the trunk.

"How come you didn't let *me* use the saw?" Aidan whines, flopping down in the snow.

"Because you're too little," Weston grunts from under the tree. "You wouldn't know how to use it."

"You don't look like *you* know how to use it!"

"Of course I do." He glares at his brother, sawing more aggressively now.

I hide a smile in my glove as I watch all this unfold. Within moments, the saw is nearly through. Weston pulls the blade out and grabs onto the trunk, giving it a firm yank to finish the job. With a splintering crack, the tree gives out and falls—

On top of him.

His brothers burst out laughing, and I can't help laughing too. I feel bad, but it's just so anticlimactic; a boy who looked so full of himself just moments ago, now trapped under a Christmas tree, nothing but his boots sticking out.

Henry and his dad go over and lift the tree off Weston. That's when I see that he is laughing too.

"See?" Aidan hollers. "You *didn't* know what you were doing!"

I rush over to Weston and kneel in the snow. "You're not hurt, are you?"

He sighs. "Only my pride."

"Don't worry. I'm sure it'll bounce back in no time."

It's nearly dark by the time we return to Weston's house. The snow is falling faster now, creating a picturesque scene out the window as we shimmy furniture around to make room for the tree. Weston helps his father carry it inside, and his mother watches the process with much trepidation, calling out warnings for them not to scrape the walls or knock things over.

Once the tree is safely situated in the living room, Mrs. Ludovico leaves us "young people" to the task of decorating it. Aidan opens a storage bin of twinkle lights and begins haphazardly yanking them out.

"Whoa, whoa, whoa, hang on there," Weston says, intervening. "You're gonna get them all tangled."

"But I want to help put them on the tree," Aidan moans. "I never get to, but I'm taller this time, so I can do it. See?" He reaches his arms up to demonstrate.

"Holy crap. You're almost tall enough to join the military." Weston grins, untangling the string of lights. "But still not tall enough to do the tippy top."

"Fiiiine, you can do that part."

"Thank you, that's very kind. First, we have to see if they even work. Cross your fingers…"

All three boys cross their fingers (on both hands) as Weston pulls the end of the lights over to an outlet and plugs it in.

A rainbow glow bursts from the floor.

"YAY!" Aidan and Noah scream in unison.

The lights are still tangled, so I help work out the kinks, and Weston uses Noah as a human spool—making him hold onto one end of the string and turn in a slow circle until he is completely wrapped in multicolored lights, like a little bioluminescent sea creature.

Weston helps Aidan string the lights, and I make minor adjustments to fill in any uneven gaps.

"Oh, right—Tessa's a perfectionist about stuff like this," Weston says. "Don't tell me you're one of those people who has a monochrome Christmas tree with all matching ornaments—"

"Of course not." I elbow him playfully. "I told you, we get a real tree."

"From a *store*."

I roll my eyes and start hanging ornaments from the bin—specifically choosing the most breakable ones, to keep them out of the younger boys' reach.

That's when my phone vibrates with a text. I pull it out of my pocket and glance at the screen.

GRANDMA:
Are you still out with Weston?

I set aside the glass bulb in my hand and type back a quick reply.

TESSA:
We're back at his house now
I'm just hanging out and helping them decorate

"Who was that?" Weston asks.

"Just Grandma," I say, hunting for a place to hang my ornament.

But before I can find a good branch, my phone buzzes again. I sigh and pick it up.

GRANDMA:
Can you be home in an hour or so?
I want us all to have dinner together

My heart sinks.

The last thing I want to do is go home for another awkward evening of not knowing what to say to Mom. Especially when I'm having such a fun time here, with Weston and his family. It's strange, but lately I've felt more comfortable at the Ludovicos' house than in my own home.

But I *did* promise Grandma I would spend some time with Mom...

I pinch my lip between my fingers, not sure what to do.

Weston catches me thinking and says, "You have to go?"

I'm about to reply with *I don't know,* when Mrs. Ludovico pokes her head into the living room and says, "Tessa, can you stay for supper?"

Perfect timing.

I smile. "I think so. I'll just have to text my grandma."

"Oh, of course. Well, let me know. You're more than welcome to stay."

"Thank you."

When she disappears back into the kitchen, I answer Grandma's message.

TESSA:
Weston's mom invited me to stay for dinner
Is that ok?
I'll be home afterward

GRANDMA:
That's fine

She sounds a bit disappointed, but all I feel is relief—knowing I've been spared at least a few torturous hours with Mom.

Weston is distracted with breaking up a squabble between Noah and Aidan, so I sneak away and find Mrs. Ludovico in the kitchen, preparing dinner.

"Grandma's alright with me staying," I say briskly. "If it's not any bother."

"Of course not, sweetie. We're always happy to have you." Mrs. Ludovico gives me a little knowing smile. "And Weston is *especially* happy to have you."

I blush, tucking a lock of hair behind my ear and glancing over my shoulder toward the living room, where Weston is now lifting Noah up like Simba to perch the star on the top of the tree.

"So, I heard your mom is visiting for Christmas."

I turn back to Mrs. Ludovico. "Yeah, she is. I haven't seen her in a year, so..."

It's totally awkward.

I don't want to tell her the awful truth, so instead I shrug, abandoning the rest of my sentence.

"You must have a lot to catch up on," Mrs. Ludovico concludes.

"I guess so." I feel a pang of guilt in my stomach, having just cunningly shirked some of this "catching up" in favor of hanging out with my boyfriend.

"Well, don't let us keep you if you want to spend time with her."

"Oh no, you're not keeping me," I assure her. "My mom and my grandma have a lot to talk about. They won't miss me."

Mrs. Ludovico looks unconvinced. "I'm sure they *will* miss you. I know I would if you were my daughter. In fact, I miss you even though you're *not* my daughter."

I wish I were, I think but don't say.

Mrs. Ludovico smiles and adds, "It's a nice change to have some female company in this house of rowdy boys."

I stifle a laugh. "I don't know how you do it."

"Do what?" Weston says, hugging me from behind.

My heart jumps, and I startle—then I smile and relax into his arms, tipping my head back to look at him. "I was just congratulating your mom on her impressive ability to put up with you."

He gives me a little pretend-hurt frown. "Don't you start ganging up on me."

"Girls have to stick together."

"That's right," Mrs. Ludovico agrees.

"What?" Weston sputters. "What the heck is this?"

I flutter my eyelashes at him. "You're a boy. You wouldn't understand."

"Because I don't understand anything about girls?"

"Exactly."

A spark of a challenge lights up in his eyes, as if I've just accused him of having no sense of adventure. "Well," he says, "I'm willing to learn."

"Then you're leaps and bounds ahead of your father," Mrs. Ludovico says, and we all laugh.

Truth be told, I'm a bit jealous of Weston for having such a graceful, sweet-tempered mother—and such a strong, protective father.

It must be nice.

I know how remarkably blessed I am to have wonderful grandparents who give me all the love I could ever need and then some. But sometimes I wonder what it would be like to have a mom and a dad who are always there for you—not because they have to be, but because they *want* to be.

I've seen the way Mrs. Ludovico loves her boys—going out of her way to make them happy, sacrificing her own comfort for their every need. She has the patience of a saint and the heart of a lion. Most of all, I love how she doesn't treat Weston any differently. She gives him responsibilities and isn't afraid to hold him accountable—even in front of me.

But no matter what, I can see that Weston respects her. He loves her. She was right by his side as he went through the most traumatic time of his life, cheering him on and supporting him—literally as well as figuratively. I can tell that their relationship is only stronger because of the pain they've both had to endure. And although no one would want to go through that kind of hell, I envy the love they forged in the fire.

No amount of "catching up" with my mother will ever give us a bond like that.

How could I put my love for you into words

when I can scarcely contain it in my heart?

I hold onto things I can't let go of

and I can't let go of you

not for all the treasure in the world

(You're worth more than all the treasure in the world)

You are the ship to my restless sea

In your arms

I am safe and warm

and truly me

The storm calms and the sun paints the sky blue

the color of your eyes

and all I can say is

I love you

and thank you

for loving me too

WESTON

DECEMBER 15

"I STILL DON'T KNOW WHAT TO GET TESSA FOR CHRISTMAS,"
I say at breakfast on Wednesday.

It's a passing thought—one I don't really expect a reply to.
Everyone is busy shoving food into their mouths. Mom is cooking, and
Dad is hidden behind a copy of the *Rockford Chronicle*.

But Noah's head pops up right away. "You should get her that
Hot Wheels racetrack with the loops—you know, that one we saw at
Walmart the last time?"

I grin, shaking my head. "She's not a big fan of Hot Wheels."

Aidan points his fork at me. "You should get her a Nerf gun! That
way she can play war with us when she comes over."

I roll my eyes. "Guys, stop. You're just telling me about all the
stuff *you* want for Christmas."

"You know what you should get her?" Henry says, with a little
shit-eating grin on his face. "A dog."

I sigh, slumping in my chair.

"Then if her grandparents don't want it, *we* can keep it!"

"I'm not gonna get her a dog, Henry."

"How about a *real* gun?" Aidan offers helpfully.

"Guys, it has to be something that she would actually want."

My brothers fall silent for a long moment, frowning as they think about it—looking about as clueless as I feel.

Then Noah's eyes light up, and he says, "How about you ask her to marry you?"

Dad chuckles from behind the newspaper, which makes my face turn red, which makes Aidan and Henry burst out laughing.

I push back my chair and stand. "I have to get ready."

❄ ❄ ❄

I'm thinking about it all day at school.

Tessa's Christmas gift, that is—not asking her to marry me.

Although that's not a bad idea.

For the *future* future.

Anyway.

My biggest problem is that I really have no idea what girls like. I think Tessa was just teasing me about "not understanding girls," but she was right.

I don't understand girls.

At all.

I've never dated before, so this is all strange and new to me. Navigating a romantic relationship is kind of like learning to walk all over again with prosthetic legs. It's hard to get the hang of it—to find your balance.

Tessa has been pretty easy so far, but only because I just act like myself around her. I'm the same person for everyone—my brothers, my parents, my friends. But now I'm starting to wonder if that's a good thing or a bad thing.

Do I treat her too much like one of my brothers?

Do I rag on her too much?

Do I annoy her?

Do I make her happy?

What could I do to make her happier?

I have no idea. And if I ask her any of these questions, she'll just say that I'm great, everything's great, because that's how she is.

And I'll be back at square one.

I need some professional help.

"Clara."

She glances up from her desk as trig is emptying out. "Yeah, Wes?"

"I have a question."

"Shoot."

"What is it you like about Kaufmann?"

She narrows her eyes at me. "What kind of a question is that?"

"I don't know. A *question* question?"

"No, there's some reason you're asking. I can tell…" She crosses her arms, a suspicious grin twitching at her lips. "Did he put you up to this?"

"What? No." I laugh. "Although, that *does* seem like something he'd do. If he had an ego that needed boosting."

Clara giggles. "Which is one of the things I like about Rudy. He has humility. Unlike *some* people."

I scoff. "Humility is highly overrated."

Clara glares. "He's also sweet and kind and considerate. Sensitive, but strong. Not a pushover. Oh, and he's *divinely* handsome."

I grunt, opening a notebook. "Well, there's no accounting for taste, I guess."

She rolls her eyes. "So why are you asking me? I need to know. Are you... writing down my answers?"

I glance up from the page. "Yeah, actually. Don't worry, I'm not gonna show anyone. It's for my own personal... research."

"Research?"

"Yeah, I thought I'd go around school asking random girls what they like about their boyfriends. Or their crushes. It's like a survey, you know? I'm gonna compare all the answers and find a common denominator."

Clara looks at me like I'm nuts. "Is this some kind of social experiment?"

"You could call it that, I guess." I snap the notebook shut and stand, shouldering my backpack. "Thanks, Clara."

Next, I track down all the other girls I know—unfortunately, I can pretty much count them on one hand.

Lindsey, from the cheer team. Bleached blonde hair, bright green eyes. I find her rifling through her open locker.

"Can I ask you a question?"

"Sure..."

"It's about Julian. You're still dating him, right?"

"Uh-huh..."

"What is it you like about him? I mean, why did you want to go out with him?"

Lindsey frowns mistrustfully at my notebook, which I'm pinning against the lockers with one hand, my pen ready to write down her answer.

"It's just a survey," I explain. "Nobody will see it but me."

"You are so strange, Weston."

"Thank you. Now tell me what you like about Julian."

Lindsey smiles and sighs romantically. "What's *not* to like? He's obviously *totally* hot. Those dazzling blue eyes... And his smile—oh my god. Kills me every time. Plus, he's, like, way taller than me, which I love, and he's got, like, the hottest arms—"

"Okay, can you give me the short version?" I cut in, a little sickened by all this detail. "What about his personality do you like?"

Lindsey slams her locker shut. "He's confident. That's a huge turn-on."

Violet from the lacrosse team agrees.

"Confidence is the hottest thing about a guy, honestly," she says, twirling a lock of her black hair. "But I don't mean cockiness. *That* does just the opposite. I really like it when a guy is just... sure of himself, you know? Assertive and bold. It's cool."

I nod, writing it down. "And... do you have someone in mind right now?"

Violet bites on a smile, tilting her head. "I might..."

"But you're not gonna tell me who."

"Nope."

I move on to Candace Hayes, the only girl on the track team who isn't afraid to laugh at me while she kicks my ass.

"You got a crush on anyone?"

"That's my business, Ludovico."

"Yeah, but I need to know. I'm doing a survey."

She quirks one eyebrow. "Sure. Sounds more like you're making a list of embarrassing confessions to post on the school website."

"What?" I sputter a laugh. "Why would I do that?"

"I don't know; why else would you take a survey?" She crosses her skinny brown arms over her chest. "Tell me the reason or I'm not answering."

I groan, dragging a hand through my hair. "It's for a friend. He wants to uncover the secrets of the female mind."

Candace doesn't look convinced. "Good luck with that."

"Come on, Hayes—please help us out. You don't have to tell me who your crush is; just tell me what you like about him."

Candace glares at me for a long moment and then says at last, "He has a good sense of humor. He makes me laugh, which is *not* something anyone can do. Plus, he's kind of hot. Washboard abs and all that."

I glance up from the page with a grin. "Is it Davis?"

"*No*," she scoffs, shoving past me. "Now get lost."

I move on to some girls I don't know. I just go around the halls, tapping on female shoulders and asking them all the same question.

The consensus is this:

"He's funny and sweet and super confident, which is *very* attractive..."

"I like how he lets me vent without trying to fix my problem. Even if he's just *pretending* to listen..."

"The most attractive thing about a guy is a great personality. Like, if he has a soft side but he's also strong and confident..."

"I like how he always compliments me and makes me feel good about myself. Oh, and he calls me *beautiful* instead of *hot*—that's a deal-breaker for me..."

I'm so busy talking to all these random girls about their (mostly nameless) crushes, I end up being late for chemistry. My partner, a new girl named Shiori, is quick to forgive my tardiness. I take the opportunity to quiz her, too.

"Are you dating anyone?"

She freezes, her eyes wide behind her safety goggles. "What?"

Crap. That came out wrong.

"Uh, I mean—" I laugh under my breath. "I'm not asking for that reason. It's... for a survey. A social experiment. I'm asking everyone."

"Oh." She smiles, blushing. "No, I'm not dating anyone."

"Do you have a crush?"

"Yes."

"You don't have to tell me who it is. I'm just curious what you like about him."

She bites her lip, looking down. "Well, he's really kind and funny and outgoing. And he's always smiling, like nothing ever gets him down. I like that. Besides, he's also... very handsome."

I jot down her answer and say, "Don't worry, he won't see this. Only I will."

Shiori looks like she's about to say something else, but then she just giggles shyly and goes back to her chemicals.

At the end of the day, I show Rudy the notebook and explain the whole social experiment. We're at his house, doing homework at his kitchen table, and now he's looking at me like I have three heads.

"You seriously went around school asking every girl about her crush?"

"Well, most of them didn't tell me who their crush was, but... yeah." I squint to read my own handwriting. "That's what Clara said about you."

Rudy is in the middle of reading it, a lovestruck smile creeping onto his face. I roll my eyes and try to take back the notebook, but he slams his hand down on it.

"I'm not done."

I groan and face-plant on the table, waiting for him to finish. The pages flip, flip, flip. Then he says, "All of this sounds like you."

"Not all of them. I don't play football—"

"Okay, whatever, but all the other ones," Rudy says. "Especially this Shiori chick. Who's that?"

"The girl I was sitting next to in lab."

Rudy frowns curiously at the page, as if suddenly noticing something weird about the responses—but he doesn't say what. Instead, he swings the notebook shut. "What I want to know is what any of this has to do with Tessa."

"Well... nothing. I just want to get a general idea of what girls find attractive. You know?"

He raises an eyebrow. "You don't think Tessa finds you attractive?"

"It's not that. It's just..." I sigh. "Look, I've never had a girlfriend before. I just want to do it right. I want to be a good boyfriend and... make this a special Christmas for her."

"Well, I don't see how this helps you decide what to get her for Christmas."

I mutter a dry laugh. "It doesn't. But that's not why I did it. I was trying to... understand girls a little better."

"And do you?"

I flip through the notebook, shaking my head. "Nope. Can't say that I do."

❄ ❄ ❄

That night, when I'm FaceTiming Tessa in bed, I decide to come right out and ask her.

"What do you want for Christmas?"

She's in the middle of brushing her teeth, and has her phone propped up on the sink. Pajamas, no makeup, hair in a sloppy bun— she's never looked more beautiful to me.

"Oh, I don't know," she says through her toothbrush. "Nothing, really. I just want to spend time with you."

That's exactly what I was afraid of.

I groan, dropping my head back into my pillows. "That doesn't help me at all."

Tessa rinses her mouth and splashes water all over her face. "Well, don't go spending a bunch of money on me, or I'll feel bad."

"Don't worry. I'm broke."

She laughs.

"And I don't mean it has to be expensive. I just meant…" I sigh, dragging a hand over my face. "I want to give you something special."

"Every moment with you is special to me," Tessa says, sounding like a holiday greeting card.

"Well, same. But…"

"But what?"

"I don't know."

I *do* know. But I'm not going to talk about it.

Not with her.

I watch her go into her room and climb into bed, snuggling under the covers. Her beautiful, smiling face glows in the lamplight.

She sighs and says, "I wish you were here."

"In bed with you? I don't think your grandparents would be too happy about that."

Tessa tries to give me a sharp look, but she's grinning too much to pull it off.

"I wish I were there, too," I say. "Even if I was just… on the floor."

She grunts a laugh.

"How was your day? With your mom?"

She shrugs. "It was okay. We went shopping, so at least I wasn't stuck in the house with her. Plus, I had my AirPods—thank the Lord. Then when we got back, I stayed in my room and did schoolwork."

"Must be nice to *choose* when you do school."

"It is. But lately I've been wishing I had a place to escape to all day."

I frown, noticing her choice of words. Just a week ago, Tessa never would have described public school as "an escape." She's always bragging about how great homeschooling is, how she wouldn't trade it for anything.

There must be way more to this mom thing than I first realized.

"Oh, so I was gonna ask you if you want to come over tomorrow after you get out of school."

"Yeah, sure," I say. "What's going on? Sounds like you've got a plan up your sleeve."

Tessa smirks. "Remember the Christmas party I was telling you about? The thing our church puts on every year? Well, I always bake something for it. So, this year I'm doing cookies—and I need lots of help."

"Which means you're outdoing yourself. As usual."

She glares. "Of course. Ten dozen cookies total."

"Ten dozen?" I nearly choke. "Why do you do this to yourself? Can't we just buy them from the store?"

"No, of course not. Store-bought cookies are blasphemy. Besides, they're no fun. I was looking forward to having some cozy romantic baking time with you."

I smile. "Sounds like a plan."

"Oh, and you're obviously invited to the church party," Tessa adds. "It's on Saturday night. We're going to go caroling around town and then hang out at the church. You know, your typical Christian gathering. It shouldn't go too late."

"Caroling, huh?"

Tessa grins. "Mm-hmm, and don't say you can't sing because I know you *can*."

It doesn't sound half as fun as baking cookies with Tessa, but if she's there, I'm sure it will be a good time.

"Alright. Count me in."

TESSA

DECEMBER 16

IT'S SNOWING AGAIN ON THURSDAY—BIG, FLUFFY FLAKES that magically transform the world into a snow globe. I have all my cookie recipes spread out on the kitchen island, ready to go.

Two dozen each of snickerdoodles, gingerbread, and chocolate crinkles, and four dozen sugar cookies. I've double-checked to be sure I have all the ingredients. There's nothing so awful as starting to bake something only to discover, halfway through the mess, that you don't have all the ingredients. I've learned that lesson the hard way, and now I always make sure I am properly supplied before I get started.

I've been looking forward to this romantic baking session all morning. The mood is set—balsam fir candles burning and a Bing Crosby Christmas album spinning on the record player in the living room.

Now all I need is my helper.

At three o'clock, I hear a car pull into the driveway, then Weston's telltale knock on the front door.

"I'll get it!" I singsong, dancing through the house and answering the door with a giddy flourish.

Weston smiles when he sees me wearing my candy cane apron. "Hey, beautiful." He leans in and gives me a quick kiss on the lips.

I melt a little as I kiss him back. "I see your mom let you borrow her car," I say, peeking outside to find the silver Acadia parked in our driveway. "Hopefully she doesn't need it—or you—for the rest of the day, because this is probably going to take a while."

Weston grins. "I'm all yours."

I drag him into the kitchen and make him wash his hands (don't even get me started on the appalling hygiene of teenage boys), and then I explain my plan.

"I was thinking we should start with the chocolate crinkle cookies because they need to chill for a few hours… Then, in the meantime, we can make the sugar cookies, then the snickerdoodles, and we can make the gingerbread last."

Weston raises his eyebrows at all the recipes spread out on the counter. "I think *I'll* need to chill for a few hours after all that."

I giggle and shove a festive red plaid apron at him—watching as he slips it on over his head. He looks so incredibly cute; I could smother him in kisses.

I'm about to, actually—but that's when Mom walks in.

"What's going on in here?" she questions, her rough voice disrupting Bing Crosby and, consequently, any fragment of romance. "Oh, hi, Weston!"

"Hey, Heather," Weston says with a genuine smile—as if he's actually *happy* to see my mother. "Tessa's recruited me to help her bake a billion cookies. And of course, she couldn't limit herself to just *one* kind"—he gives me a pointed look—"because she's one of these people who has to make everything more complicated."

I shoot him a glare in jest.

74

Then Mom's eyes light up, and she says, "I'll help you guys!"

My stomach plummets. "What?"

"Well, it looks like you have your work cut out for you."

"Yeah, we sure do," Weston says, turning to me with an unruffled smile. "Your mom can do the chocolate ones while we get started on the other stuff."

I glare at him again—and this time it's *not* in jest.

He frowns, like *What's wrong?*

Mom starts presumptuously stringing herself into an apron. "As long as I'm not intruding…"

"Course not," Weston answers for me, setting my teeth on edge.

Well, there goes our romantic time together.

I trudge back to the cupboard and grab some extra mixing bowls for Mom. I begin talking her through the directions for the chocolate crinkle cookies, but she assures me that she doesn't need any help.

"I *have* made cookies before, honey."

I press an annoyed smile onto my lips. "Good." I leave Mom at the island and go back to the counter, where Weston is waiting for my direction. We start on the sugar cookies, using an old recipe that Grandma inherited from *her* mother. The secret ingredient is confectioners' sugar instead of regular sugar.

I start measuring flour and try to ignore Mom, who is now talking to Weston—about herself, of course. But at least she's not asking him impertinent questions today. I don't know how he can just brush off what happened last time and act so comfortable and chill around me. I still have a bad taste in my mouth from that first meeting, and I wasn't even the recipient of her insults.

Weston is definitely a better person than me.

"So," he says at one point, "tell me what Tessa was like as a little kid."

How would my mother know? She wasn't here.

"Oh, she was as quiet as can be," Mom says, laughing, as if she actually remembers my childhood. "And she was such an orderly little perfectionist, even back then. I remember when Ma and I used to be in the kitchen, she'd be sitting in the pantry over there, rearranging all the spices."

Weston grins. "Sounds like Tessa."

"Oh, and she *hated* to go outside. If it was cold or windy, she'd be bawling her little eyes out until I took her back in."

That makes Weston laugh and loop his arms around my waist. "You haven't changed a bit."

I smack him playfully. "Shut up."

Weston turns back to Mom and says, "When I first met Tessa, it took me over a *month* to convince her to go outside."

"Oh my god!" Mom says with a raspy laugh. "That's so funny."

"It wasn't, really," I mutter. "There was a reason I didn't want to go outside. I was blind."

Weston gives me a wink. "Small details."

Mom starts asking him more about what happened over the summer, how we met, etcetera, and he tells so many stories with such funny commentary that in any other circumstance, I would enjoy it. But right now, everything is getting on my nerves.

Mom's raucous laughter.

The mess that's only getting bigger.

The music in the other room.

The fact that I'm doing most of the work myself at this point, and it's hard to concentrate on the recipe with all this chatter and noise.

I bottle up my annoyance, dropping dishes into the sink with a heavy hand. "Mom, are you done with that dough? If so, it needs to be wrapped in plastic and go in the fridge for a few hours."

"Oh, okay…"

"And, Weston, can you help me clear off the counter? It's a mess. I shouldn't be the only one doing this." I heave a sigh, digging through the cupboard in search of cookie cutters.

I hate snapping at Weston, especially when it's not his fault that this whole experience is going down the tubes—but I just can't stand how I seem to be the only one taking this seriously.

"Hey," Weston says quietly to me, "I thought this was supposed to be fun."

I sigh. "Yeah, well, at this rate, it's going to be midnight before all the cookies are done."

"What can I do to help?"

Get rid of Mom, I think but don't say. "Um, you can start rolling these out. I'll find the baking sheets."

While I dig through yet *more* cabinets, Mom starts doing the dishes. I wish she would just leave them for me to do, but there's no stopping her from lavishing her "help" on me. Truth be told, I would rather wash all the dishes myself than listen to her talk for one more minute.

I busy myself with cutting the sugar cookies and arranging them on trays, intermittently smacking Weston's hand away from the bowl as he tries to steal cookie dough behind my back.

Finally, Mom says she needs a smoke and goes outside—leaving us alone, at last. I slide the first batch of sugar cookies into the oven and set the timer, muttering under my breath, "I hope she smokes the whole pack."

Weston laughs, taking my shoulders and pulling me into a hug. "Can you lighten up a little?"

I stiffen, annoyed, even with his warm, comforting arms circled around me. "I'm perfectly light," I snap. "If I were any lighter, I would be… floating off the ground!"

Weston grins, looking down at me with a spark of mischief in his eyes. "Like this?" He grabs my waist and lifts me off my feet.

I gasp. "Weston!"

He sets me on the counter with an exaggerated grunt. "Yep," he says. "You're heavy. You need to lighten up."

A laugh spills out of me despite everything. "You are hateful," I whisper, running my fingers through his hair.

"Not as hateful as you are," he murmurs. His hands rest on my hips as he studies my face, his gaze soft but serious. "Your mom is just trying to be nice."

"Well, so am I."

He lifts his eyebrows, like *Are you kidding?*

My jaw clenches, but I keep my voice low. "She's kind of insufferable sometimes, don't you think? I *specifically* didn't invite her to do the cookies with us because I knew she'd just talk about herself the whole time, and I wanted to have a nice romantic baking session, just the two of us. But no, she had to barge in and ruin every—"

He kisses me, silencing my words. I know he only does it to make me shut up, which is so infuriating I could smack him—but that's kind of hard to do when all my insides have turned to mush. Weston's kisses tend to make my whole body go weak.

A rush of love spreads through me like warm sunlight as his hands gently squeeze my hips, making my heart flutter like crazy. My lips move in a dance with his, and my fingers curl through his hair, and for a moment, I forget anything else exists…

Then Mom walks in.

"Oh, so *this* is what happens when I leave the room!"

I break away from Weston's lips, my heart jumping out of my chest, my cheeks blushing hot.

Mom stands in the doorway, smirking.

"Uh, no—" I stammer. "No, it doesn't, usually… just—"

"It's all good, honey," Mom says with an exaggerated wink. "Don't let me interrupt!" She darts out of the room again as quickly as she appeared.

Weston stifles a laugh. "Sorry. I couldn't resist."

I lean close to his ear and smile. "I'm glad you didn't."

❄ ❄ ❄

When all the cookies are done, I'm exhausted. I never knew baking could take so much out of you. I feel like I've just finished running a marathon, and now all I want to do is cuddle Weston and watch a Hallmark movie.

Once the kitchen is cleaned up, that's exactly what we do. Mom and Grandma have gone out to spend some time together, and Grandpa is visiting a church member at the hospital, so it's just me and Weston alone in the house.

Finally.

I gather the fluffiest pillows and the coziest blanket, turn the TV on soft, and flop down on the couch with Weston. I have him take off his prosthetic legs so that I can snuggle him without anything in the way, and he's happy to oblige.

"God, it feels good to ditch those things." He sighs, leaning back against the pillows and shutting his eyes. He looks so adorable.

I smile, snuggling up close to him and laying my head on his chest. He loops one arm around my back, and *Lord*, he smells so good, it makes me want to stay here forever. There is nothing cozier than the feeling of being held in Weston's arms as the snow falls outside and a Hallmark Christmas movie murmurs on the TV.

"I'm sorry about earlier," I say softly, spreading my hand over his chest. "I'm sorry for being a…"

"Cookie Nazi?"

I roll my eyes. "Actually, I was looking for another word."

"The one that rhymes with 'itch'?"

I groan a laugh, pinching my eyes shut. "Yeah. That."

He chuckles, kissing the top of my head. "It's okay. I knew you were stressed out."

"I just had all these expectations, you know?"

"Mm-hmm. You always do."

I sigh. "I didn't mean to be rude to Mom."

"But you wish she wasn't here," Weston observes rather bluntly.

"It's not that. I just don't understand *why* she's here. I know she says that she wants to spend time with me, but… she never wanted to before. What makes her think she can just start being a mother when she feels like it?"

Weston goes quiet for a minute, rubbing his thumb gently against my arm. "Maybe she's had a change of heart."

"I doubt it."

"You don't think people can change?"

"I don't think *Mom* can change," I contend. "Not that much, anyway. She's always been selfish and irresponsible. And yeah, she's here now, but what about after Christmas? She'll have had her fill of being a mom, and then she'll go back to Pittsburgh, and everything will go back to the way it was before. So what's the point in all this mother-daughter bonding time? You know?"

"Yeah, I get you," Weston murmurs thoughtfully, his voice

getting sleepier. "But everyone deserves a second chance."

"I guess so."

"You gave *me* a second chance, and look what happened."

I grin, tipping my head back to look at him. "I didn't give you a second chance, actually. You just kept persisting until I finally gave up."

Weston laughs under his breath and pulls me closer. "That's 'cause I knew you were a keeper."

WESTON

DECEMBER 16

I WAKE UP TO PINS AND NEEDLES IN MY RIGHT ARM. Something smells amazing, like strawberries or roses—and there's a TV murmuring quietly nearby. It all makes sense to me when I open my eyes.

Tessa is asleep in my arms, her sweet-smelling hair spilling over my chest, her breathing soft and steady. It's dark outside the window, but I have no idea what time it is. Even if I could get up to check, I wouldn't want to. Tessa looks so peaceful; I can't wake her.

Before we dozed off, she was talking about her mom—all the reasons she doesn't want to hang out with her. I suspected there was some unresolved crap between them, but now I'm starting to see that it's all on Tessa's side.

She's holding onto a grudge, I can tell. This isn't just about the future—not about her mom leaving after Christmas and things going back to the way they were.

This is about the past.

Tessa is hurting. I could hear it in her voice when she talked about her mom being "selfish and irresponsible." She said it in that fancy, smart-mouth way of hers, but there was a little kid underneath—the Tessa who used to rearrange the spices and cry if it was too cold outside.

The Tessa her mom left behind.

I know it must suck—and I can't pretend to understand what it's like. But I want to help. As far as I can see, Tessa's mom is trying to make it up to her, trying to start over. I get Tessa's caution, but she's not even giving this thing a chance.

I wish I could give her some advice, but I don't know how to do that without offending her. I'm afraid she'll take it the wrong way, and the last thing I want to do is start an argument and ruin our Christmas together—especially when it's really none of my business.

I decide it's better to steer clear of any potentially hazardous topics. Support Tessa and fight in her corner. Listen to her vent without trying to fix the problem.

Be the best boyfriend ever.

That's when the front door opens and Mrs. Dickinson's voice comes spilling inside—along with Heather's smoky laughter. Tessa stirs in my arms, pulling in a deep breath and nuzzling her face into my neck.

"What time is it?" she murmurs, her voice all groggy and cute.

"Time for me to go home, I think."

"*Nooo*," she moans, and wraps her arms tighter around me like a sloth hugging a tree. "Don't go yet."

"Your grandma's gonna catch us sleeping together in a minute," I whisper, which makes her laugh in this silly, love-drunk way.

"I don't care," she hisses into my ear. "I'll hide your prosthetic legs so that you can't leave."

"That… is a great idea."

Mrs. Dickinson snaps on a light in the living room. "Oh. There you are. Weston's still here?"

"Mm-hmm." Tessa hugs me tighter. "And he's not leaving."

I laugh, rubbing her back. "I have to. Or my mom might revoke my driver's license."

❄ ❄ ❄

Later that night when I'm home and finishing up an overdue psych paper, Mom pokes her head into my bedroom.

"You busy?"

"Not really." I turn around in my desk chair to face her. "What's up?"

"I want to talk to you about something," Mom says, and shuts the door. "Alone."

I freeze, worried. "Oh yeah? Did I… do something wrong?"

"No, no. It's not you. It's about Henry."

"Henry?"

Mom nods. "Your father and I were talking, and…" She breaks into a smile. "We're thinking of getting him a puppy for Christmas."

"Are you serious?"

"Yes, and I'm probably crazy too, but… he so badly wants a dog. And he seems very serious about taking on the responsibility of looking after it."

I grin, shaking my head. "I knew you'd cave. I thought: if anyone can convince Mom to get a dog, it's Henry. 'Cause he's your favorite."

"I don't have favorites," Mom insists, and I'm not sure which of us she's trying to convince. "But Henry *is* mature for his age, so I think he can handle this. Dad and I have discussed it at length. Someone at the ,*Chronicle* knows a lady whose golden retriever just had puppies a couple of months ago."

"That's convenient," I say, trying not to laugh. "I'm surprised they're not all taken."

"Well… your father had her hold one for us, a while ago."

"What? You've been planning this for months? God! He is *definitely* your favorite."

Mom laughs. "Shhh—stop saying that. Now, this is where I need your help. We're going to have to keep it a secret until Christmas morning."

"Mm. Yeah, I'm pretty sure you can't put a puppy in a box under the tree."

"Exactly. So, I was wondering if Tessa and her grandparents would be willing to keep it at their house—you know, just for a few days."

"Oh, yeah. I'm sure they'd be cool with that."

"Well, don't *assume*. You have to ask."

I sigh, grabbing my phone. "Okay, I'll ask right now."

WESTON:
Henry won
We're getting him a puppy
Top secret

      TESSA:
      !!!!!!!!
      OMG
      I'M SO HAPPY RIGHT NOW

WESTON:

ur gonna be even happier in a minute

mom wants u guys to take care of it until xmas

> **TESSA:**
> WHAT

WESTON:

That ok?

> **TESSA:**
> YES YES YES
> But I have to ask my grandparents lol
> Hold on

Ten minutes later…

> **TESSA:**
> They said that's fine!
> As long as I clean up after it

WESTON:

ur the best

> **TESSA:**
> Can I come with you to pick it up?

WESTON:

HELL yes

lol my phone automatically capitalizes cuss words ;)

TESSA:
why am I not surprised

WESTON:
Sunday afternoon
that good with u?

TESSA:
Can't wait!!!

WESTON:
We'll pretend we're going on a date or something

TESSA:
Sounds perfect
I'll wear something cute for authenticity

WESTON:
not too cute
in case the dog pees on it

TESSA

DECEMBER 18

I HAVE NO CLUE WHAT TO GIVE WESTON FOR CHRISTMAS.
I've been thinking about it for weeks—turning over dozens of ideas in
my mind. But so far, nothing has struck me as special enough. This
will be our first Christmas together, and I want to make it
unforgettable. My mother's unexpected visit has probably done that
already—in the worst way—but even now, I think I can make this
holiday special for us.

Even if it's not the *best* Christmas ever.

At this point, I need to focus on the things I *can* control, like
spending time with Weston and finding the perfect gift for him.

The problem is, I'm completely out of ideas—even when it comes
to dates. He's the spontaneous one, always pushing me outside my
comfort zone. Fun doesn't come naturally to me—I have to search for
it on Pinterest. And even then, I have a hard time knowing what
actually *is* fun until I'm doing it.

Am I too dull for Weston? He's so charismatic, so adventurous—
so unlike me. They say opposites attract, but do they last? Does an

effervescent guy like Weston eventually get tired of an unexciting girl like me?

I don't know.

The thought of it makes me nervous. I'm as happy as can be just staying home with him, baking cookies and snuggling on the couch. But he would probably rather be doing some daredevil thing, like skiing or skydiving.

Weston joked about being the best boyfriend I've ever had—and although I have no one else to compare him to, I know that he *is* the best. Sometimes, I can't believe how blessed I am to call him *mine*. There must be so many girls who wish they could say the same.

I ponder all of this on Saturday as I help get everything ready for the church party. Grandma and I safely transport all ten dozen meticulously assorted cookies to the church, where we help the worship team set up tables in the foyer for refreshments. Jolly paper bunting adorns the walls, and a stout Christmas tree sparkles on one side of the room, standing guard over a pile of gifts wrapped and ready to be donated to children at the hospital.

Pulling off a well-organized Christmas party is the pride and joy of our church—a tradition Grandpa has been carrying out since I was a little girl. Every year, we assemble on a cold night in December to sing and talk and laugh and drink cocoa and eat way too many cookies. We also perform a live nativity scene on the green, which I spent my childhood devotedly participating in—dressed up in glittery angel's wings and a silky white robe. When I turned thirteen, I decided I was too old (and too cold) to be an angel anymore, and resorted to baking cookies for the party instead.

By the time we finish setting up, it's nearly dark out. Grandma and I head back home to eat something and get ready for the party.

Weston is coming over at eight o'clock, and we're driving down to the church together. I've already done my makeup, so all I have to do is curl my hair and change into the outfit I've already planned in my head: gray leggings and a long Nordic funnel-neck sweater with my fuzzy leather boots.

When I come downstairs, Grandma says, "You're going to freeze like that."

I sigh. "No, I won't. This sweater is super warm."

"Bring a jacket."

"Alright…"

But I won't wear it.

That's when Mom steps into the room, wearing jeans and a maroon fleece jacket. She looks marginally more put-together than usual.

My heart sinks a little as I realize what this means. "Oh… you're coming? I thought you said you didn't want to."

Mom blinks at me. "Well, I don't *have* to."

"No, you should come, Heather," Grandma says, rummaging through the coat closet for her parka.

"I don't know…" Mom murmurs, shifting uncomfortably. "You guys would probably have more fun without me. I don't really know anybody from your church, and… I'd probably just get in the way."

Grandma is about to argue when three fast knocks come from the front door.

Weston.

I dart over and swing the door open. There stands Weston, looking like a very handsome country boy in his Carhartt jacket and jeans.

I smile. "You're here, thank goodness—"

"Five minutes early, too," he says, stepping inside and sweeping me off my feet. I gasp, laughing as he twirls me around and kisses the top of my head. "You look beautiful. Mm, how do you always make your hair smell so good? Oh, hi, Mom."

Mom chuckles. "Hi, Weston."

"Everyone ready to go?" Weston asks.

"Uh, well, Mom isn't sure if she wants to come," I say, looping one arm around Weston.

"What?" He looks shocked. "You gotta come, Heather."

She laughs a little, unsure. "I don't know… I'm not much of a churchgoer."

"Me neither," Weston says. "But Tessa assures me that heathens are welcome." He smirks and winks at me.

Mom still doesn't look convinced that she *is* welcome, but before she can refuse, Weston adds, "Besides, you helped us make the cookies. You deserve to eat some of them." He gives my mother his most heart-melting smile, and who could possibly say no to that face?

I want to stomp on his foot—I would, if he could feel it.

Why is he doing this? Is he *trying* to ruin my night?

Mom gives in. "Oh, alright. You twisted my arm," she says with a raspy laugh. "Who knows? It might be fun."

Not for me.

A flare of irritation rises in my chest, but I shove it down and force a joyless smile onto my face.

It was awkward enough having Mom with us last Sunday at church, but the party will be even worse. I'll get more questions and have to put on a show, pretending that we're one big happy family when we are just the opposite.

Honestly, Weston—couldn't you have kept your nose out of my business for *once*?

WESTON

DECEMBER 18

THE NIGHT GETS OFF TO A ROCKY START. TESSA SEEMS annoyed before we even leave her house, which I can only assume has something to do with her mom. She's no less of a volcano than the day I first met her—and over the past six months, I've learned to predict her eruptions of righteous anger.

There might be one coming tonight.

When we get to the church, there's already a crowd of people milling around outside—candles and Christmas sweaters everywhere. I notice a little shack set up on the lawn with a couple huddled inside, dressed up like Mary and Joseph—a real baby wailing in the girl's arms and a real donkey chilling in the snow, looking annoyed.

Tessa reintroduces me to some of her friends, people I met over the summer but whose names I've forgotten. We exchange small talk for a while until someone rustles up a band of carolers, and Tessa drags me along with them.

It's the first time I've ever done something like this, but Tessa helps me to not feel totally like a fish out of water. With her hand in mine and her beautiful smiling face beside me, I feel confident belting out the wrong lyrics to Christmas songs in the middle of the street.

Whenever I start laughing, Tessa starts laughing—which makes her smack me because I'm ruining her Perfect Church Girl appearance. I learn that her favorite Christmas song is "Auld Lang Syne," and make a mental note to learn that one on the ukulele.

About halfway through our caroling route, I notice that Tessa is shivering.

"You cold?"

"I left my jacket in the car," she whimpers, hugging me for warmth.

I slip off my jacket and wrap it around her. "Here, put this on."

"Oh, you don't have to—"

"Shh. I want all the girls to be jealous of you."

She giggles and zips up the jacket, nuzzling the collar. "I love you."

I put my arm around her shoulders and kiss the top of her head. "I love you more."

Tessa's mom is somewhere in the group, but she doesn't talk to us the whole time. Probably because Tessa is glued to my side, and her mom feels awkward hanging back with us—like a third wheel.

I feel bad for her. Tessa has been giving her the cold shoulder all night, even though I haven't heard her say anything to piss Tessa off. I guess she's just angry that her mom is here at all.

Something about it doesn't sit right with me. Shouldn't she at least *act* like they're related?

I start to feel like a distraction. If I weren't here, Tessa would probably be hanging out with her mother.

When we get closer to the church, I decide to say something about it.

"We don't have to be in each other's pockets the whole time, you know."

I say it as gently as I know how, but Tessa still whips around to look at me with a startled expression.

"What?"

"I mean, you should probably spend some time with your mom."

She grunts. "No thanks."

We come to a stop on the green, where the carolers are now mingling with the rest of the crowd, talking and laughing. Puffs of steam in the candlelight.

God, it's fricking cold.

But I won't ask for my jacket back—that's about the most unromantic thing a guy can do. Instead, I stand here and freeze, watching Tessa. She's staring at the nativity scene, but I can tell she's thinking about what I just said.

Finally, she turns to me, her voice razor-sharp. "Why did you have to encourage her to come, anyway? She didn't want to come."

"She *did* want to come," I say. "She just thought *you* didn't want her to come."

"Well, maybe I didn't."

"Why?"

"Because!" Tessa snaps, her eyes flashing. "I wanted to have a good time, not spend the whole night faking smiles and pretending Mom and I have this great relationship when we don't."

"Maybe you could," I argue, "if you tried. And then you wouldn't have to fake your smiles."

"It's not as easy as that. It's too late to…" Tessa's voice fades, and she looks away, shaking her head. "Why do you care so much about this, anyway?"

"Because I want you to be happy."

"I *am* happy."

"You don't look it."

"Well, I'm sorry I'm not as *chipper* as you are all the time! You know, it's easy for you—"

"Oh, of course," I mutter dryly. "It's *easy* for me."

"Yeah. It is. Because you have a mother who loves you and your brothers more than anything in this world. She would probably cut off her own arm for you."

"Nice analogy."

"Ugh—you know what I mean! She would sacrifice her *life* for you." Tessa's voice wobbles, and I catch a glint of tears in her eyes. "My mom wouldn't sacrifice *anything* for me. That's why she left."

I don't know what to say.

This topic isn't headed anywhere good—I should never have brought it up. And to make matters worse, I'm starting to feel things below my knees. Weird, tingling sensations in the parts of me that aren't even there.

I pull in a deep breath, ignoring it. "Look, Tessa. I know you're finding it hard to forgive your mom for what she did—"

"How can I forgive her when she never even said she was sorry?"

"She's *trying* to. Can't you see that? God, I don't even know the woman and even I can see that she's trying—"

"That's right," Tessa snaps, getting right in my face. "You *don't* know her. So why are you taking her side?"

I stare at her, speechless, for a moment. "I didn't know there were sides," I say quietly.

"Well, there *are*. And I thought you'd be on mine." She looks so betrayed when she says that, it feels like a knife in my chest. She turns away sharply, crossing her arms. Stubborn as hell.

"Tessa, I'm always on your side. It's just—"

A bolt of pain suddenly rips through me.

Holy shit.

My legs are burning, like I just walked through a fire. It's savage, familiar, maddening. I grimace, pressing my eyes shut and swallowing a moan of pain.

"I can't fight with you about this," I say, and turn away.

I have to get warm.

I head for the church, weaving around clusters of people and trying to hold it together—telling myself, *It's okay. You're fine. Just get inside.*

The lobby of the church is loud with voices and laughter—everyone is crowded around the tables, eating and drinking. I cut through the mob, my legs still burning, and shoulder open the door to the sanctuary.

It's empty. Thank God.

Muttering cusses under my breath, I take a seat in one of the pews facing the invisible preacher. I warm my hands up by rubbing them together, then I start massaging my stumps where my prostheses meet my legs.

I close my eyes and take deep breaths, trying to focus on the sensation of warmth—not the pain my body is tricking me into feeling.

Tessa's voice keeps replaying in my head—haunting me, even in the silence of this empty church.

"Why are you taking her side?… I thought you'd be on mine."

Damn it.

I should have known she'd take it the wrong way. Why did I have to go and open my big mouth?

Now she's mad at me.

Nice job, Weston.

This is exactly what I was afraid of: the mom issue getting between us, because Tessa is just as stubborn as I am. I can't keep my opinions to myself. And she can hold a grudge like nobody's business.

But I *am* on her side—how can I make her see that?

Suddenly, the door opens behind me, letting in a burst of noise from the lobby—

And Tessa's mom.

"There you are," she says, smiling hesitantly as she steps in. "Is everything okay?"

I shrug, not wanting to lie and not wanting to tell the truth either. I'm still rubbing my knees, though most of the pain has subsided at this point, leaving a dull ache in its place.

"Are your legs hurting you?" Heather asks, taking a seat beside me in the pew.

"Nah, not really. Just some phantom pain."

"Phantom pain?" She looks clueless. "What is that?"

Sometimes I forget that most people have never heard of it.

"Uh, well, basically it's my brain doing a security check," I explain. "And my nervous system security guards forget that I had my legs amputated, so when they get to *that* part, they freak out. It's like a Code Red alert goes off in my brain, which doesn't really know what the hell is going on, so it just assumes the worst and sends out excruciating pain signals to make sense of it." I pause, managing a weak smile. "At least, that's how I explain it to my little brothers."

Heather shakes her head slowly. "That's awful."

"Yeah, it sucks. But it doesn't happen too much anymore. Cold triggers it sometimes. That's why I came in here."

"Oh." Heather nods, looking somewhat relieved. "I thought maybe you and Tessa had an argument. I saw you talking, and... Well, it's none of my business of course, but... I just hope it wasn't about me."

I look at the floor, not knowing how to answer that one.

But my silence is answer enough.

She gets it—I can tell by the heavy sigh. "I shouldn't have come."

"Of course you should have."

"That's not what I mean," Heather murmurs. "I'm not talking about tonight or this party... I mean I shouldn't have come at all."

I can't argue there. Sad as it is, she's probably right. Seems like this holiday visit hasn't been much fun for anyone so far.

"I wasn't expecting Tessa to be *excited* to see me," she says. "But I thought we'd at least get a chance to talk, you know? I wanted to make up for lost time. But now I'm starting to think it was a mistake. 'Cause she sure doesn't want to see *me*... I guess it's been too long. I've missed my chance." She pushes a lifeless smile onto her face, nodding in glum acceptance.

I don't say anything; I just think about it from her perspective—something that Tessa should try sometime.

Heather laughs a little nervously and says, "Sorry, hon—I don't mean to dump all this on you. Ignore me. I'll be gone soon enough. And Tessa will be glad to see the back of me."

She doesn't know Tessa.

She doesn't know that *glad* is the last thing Tessa will be to watch her mother walk away again.

It's none of my business.

I should keep my opinions to myself.

But I can't sit here and let her believe a lie.

So I come right out and say, "Can I give you some advice?"

"Of course." Heather waits with genuine interest, as if I'm about to unload some complex wisdom for her.

Really, I just have one word.

"Stay."

She frowns, taken aback. "Stay? After Christmas?"

"You said you were out of work, right? Well, why don't you get a job here, in Rockford? Why don't you move here?"

Heather blinks. "I... don't think that's a good idea. Tessa can barely stand me staying for the holidays. I don't think she'd be too thrilled about me moving here permanently."

I shake my head. "No, see, that's where you're wrong. Tessa doesn't want you to leave. I know it seems like that, but... I know her pretty well by this point. She doesn't like letting her guard down. It's not because she doesn't love you—she *does* love you. She's just afraid of losing you. Losing your love."

I feel gutted after saying those words, and at first, I don't know why—but it's like I just cut open my chest and let her see something that I've been hiding in the dark. My voice comes out sounding choked. "It scares her more than she'll ever say."

That's when I realize I'm not talking about Tessa.

I'm talking about myself.

And Heather knows. The light shifts in her eyes, and she sees right through me.

I turn away before she can see anything else.

Like the tears beginning to sting in my eyes.

I look down, feeling Heather's gaze on the side of my face. Her voice is quiet and sympathetic when she speaks again. "*You're* afraid of losing her, aren't you?"

I can't reply.

Not with this fricking lump in my throat.

All I can do is nod.

"Why?"

I breathe a lifeless laugh. "Take a guess."

Heather looks at me, stunned. "You can't believe Tessa would break up with you because of your legs. It sounds so ridiculous, just saying it out loud."

"I know—it does, but…" I lean forward on my knees, hanging my head. "I don't know."

"It's not *that* big a deal," she says. "I mean, it doesn't seem to stop you from doing much. And as far as the love life goes, you guys can still have all the fun other couples have."

It takes a second to click for me, and when it does, I laugh—caught off guard. My face instantly turns red.

"Oops, there goes my big mouth again…"

I grin. "I like you, Heather. I like how you always speak your mind."

"Well, you'd be the first," she says with a weary chuckle. "I know Tessa hates that about me."

"She doesn't like it about me, either. And that's part of why I worry. She gets so mad at me when I tell her the truth, but I can't lie, y'know?" I sigh, looking down at my hands. "Sometimes I feel like I'm too much. And not enough. All at the same time."

Heather goes quiet for a second, then I feel her hand on my shoulder, and I glance up into her eyes. "You're forgetting one thing."

"What's that?"

"Tessa loves you," she says, and it's like a sucker punch that makes me feel even more like crying. "It's as plain as the noonday sun. You make her smile in a way no one else can. She wants to spend every waking minute with you, for Pete's sake. And like you said, she doesn't let her guard down for just anybody. You've won her heart, Weston. And I can tell it was no easy task."

"No." I laugh, my voice all choked up. "No, it sure as hell wasn't. But I loved every minute of it. I loved *her*—from the moment I first met her."

"When she screamed at you?"

I nod, smiling at the memory of our first encounter. "She was stubborn as hell—still is. You have to kind of force your affection on her to prove that you really care. Then, just when you think it'll never work, she starts to take you seriously."

Her mom considers this theory for a minute—probably thinking about her own relationship with Tessa. Then she turns to me and says, "That should go to show that you are *more* than enough. Tessa's lucky to have you—and she *knows it*, too. Trust her. Trust yourself."

I pull in a shaky breath, about to thank her for that when—

The door opens behind us.

It's Tessa this time, looking high-fashion in my too-big Carhartt jacket, her cheeks rosy from the cold and her eyes sparkling as they lock on mine.

Heather stands up. "Well, I'll leave you to it." She passes me a little knowing smile and walks away—leaving Tessa and me alone in the big, empty church.

"I was wondering where you went," she says, sitting down beside me.

"I was cold," I reply, but that's it. I don't tell her about the phantom pain. There's no reason to, really. She'd just feel bad for me.

I hate people feeling bad for me.

I hate being different.

"You should have told me," Tessa says, with guilt in her eyes. "I would have given you back your jacket."

I manage a wry smirk. "That would kind of ruin my 'considerate boyfriend' image, I think."

Tessa laughs under her breath, then falls silent as she looks up at the empty pulpit. A long silence swells between us, and I hope she doesn't bring up the conversation we never finished outside. I don't want to fight with her, and I don't want to lie, either. If we can't be on the same page, I'd rather just close the book.

"I remember coming in here one year during the party," Tessa murmurs. "I must've been seven or eight years old. I was an angel in the nativity scene, and one of my wings fell off outside, and I couldn't find it. I was bawling my eyes out, so upset... until Grandma brought me in here and fed me cookies. It solved everything."

I laugh, because she is the cutest person I've ever met—despite her volcanic eruptions of righteous anger. I put my arm around her, pulling her in closer to kiss her temple; she giggles and rests her head on my shoulder.

"I'm sorry," I whisper into her hair.

"Me too." She reaches down and grabs my hand, threading her fingers through mine. "Let's not fight... ever again."

I smile. "Okay."

But I know that we *will* fight again.

And I'm scared we won't make it out of the next one like this.

TESSA

DECEMBER 19

AFTER CHURCH ON SUNDAY, MY GRANDPARENTS DROP ME off at Weston's house for Operation Puppy. I ring the doorbell, and Mrs. Ludovico greets me within moments.

"Hello, Tessa!" she says with a smile. "Come on in. I'm almost ready…"

We agreed on our cover story ahead of time: Weston's mom needs to run some errands in town, so she's going to drop him and me off somewhere for our "date," then pick us up later.

It all seems rather sneaky and deceptive, but I don't mind. When it comes to surprise Christmas gifts, the ends justify the means.

I find Weston in the kitchen with his brothers, making a (rather apocalyptic) mess. It looks like a cookie-baking escapade that was initially started by Mrs. Ludovico and overtaken by her reckless boys. Flour everywhere, dirty bowls piled in the sink, no timers going for the oven even though I can smell something baking.

"What's going on in here?" I say from the doorway, not sure if I can bear to venture any farther.

Weston looks up and smiles when he sees me. "Oh no—here comes the Cookie Nazi."

I roll my eyes, then stride in and smack him—even though I really want to kiss him. "Are you ready to go?"

"Uh, yeah. I just have to go change my shirt, 'cause Noah got *flour* all over me…" He pokes his little brother in the ear, which makes Noah erupt into a fit of giggles.

I laugh. "Well, go on, then."

Weston leaves the room, and while he's gone, I take the opportunity to be a control freak—checking on the cookies that are close to burning in the oven, setting a timer for the next tray, tidying the countertops, etcetera. I also take the opportunity to ask his brothers something only they might know the answer to.

"Hey, while Weston's not here," I say, lowering my voice conspiratorially, "I want to ask you guys… What should I get him for Christmas?"

"A Nerf gun!" Aidan replies immediately, with gusto. "You know, the one that's like an automatic rifle?" He begins imitating the sound of machine-gun fire, his fingers pointed threateningly at his brothers.

I frown. "That's not actually what Weston wants, right?"

"Well, that's what he's getting *you* for Christmas. So that we can all play war!"

My gaze shifts to Henry, who is slouched at the island, reading a book. "He's just bullshitting you," he says.

"Mommy says no cussing!" Noah screams, slapping the counter and sending up a small explosion of flour.

Henry sighs and goes back to his book. "You should get Wes a dog. Since he's the oldest. Mom would probably let *him* have one."

I try to hide my smile. "And… what would you name a dog? If he were yours."

Henry grins, and I can tell he's already thought about it—a lot. "Thor," he says decidedly.

"Mm. I bet I can guess your favorite Avenger."

"Actually, my favorite Avenger is Captain America, but it would be kind of weird to name your dog Captain America."

I laugh. "Good point."

"Is someone talking about the MCU without me?" Weston says, reentering the room wearing a different T-shirt and a betrayed expression on his face.

"Yep," I answer briskly, rubbing it in. Thanks to him, I now know that MCU is the Marvel Cinematic Universe.

Weston has been making me watch all the Marvel movies, in chronological order—to "culture" me, he says. Simultaneously, I've been forcing him to watch all my favorite period dramas and classics. He tends to fall asleep during the "boring parts," and I tend to kiss him and play with his hair during all the belligerent superhero fight scenes.

"Are you two ready?" Mrs. Ludovico says, sweeping into the kitchen to remove the cookies from the oven. "Henry, keep an eye on your brothers—and call me if you need anything. Alright?"

Henry nods, looking unenthused to be the designated babysitter.

If only he knew the *real* reason we're leaving him behind.

❄ ❄ ❄

Mrs. Ludovico knocks on the painted red door, which is adorned with an expensive-looking wreath. The whole house looks expensive, actually—a modern gray Hampton-style home with a cobblestone walkway leading up to the front porch.

The red door swings open, and a short woman with curly black hair appears with a smile.

"You must be Laura," she says, reaching out to Weston's mom for a handshake. "I'm Michelle. And these must be your kids—I'm sorry, I can't remember their names."

"My son Weston," Mrs. Ludovico introduces us. "And Tessa isn't mine—not yet, anyway."

"Ahhh," Michelle says with a knowing smirk. "I see."

We both laugh awkwardly, blushing; Weston puts his arm around me.

"Well, come on in," Michelle says, beckoning us inside the Pinterest-worthy house. She leads the way through a doorway and down a flight of stairs into the finished basement, which features a sprawling game room complete with a pool table and wet bar.

"My husband has been sharing his man cave with the puppies," Michelle explains with a chuckle. "Needless to say, he's looking forward to them going to their new homes."

I spot them immediately—a swarm of fuzzy golden puppies all yipping and stumbling over each other at the other side of the room, which is wisely gated off from the carpeted area. Their mother lies on a dog bed nearby, looking worn out by her babies.

"Oh my gosh, they're so adorable," I croon. "Can I cuddle them?"

"Yeah, go right ahead," Michelle says with a dismissive swat of her hand. Weston and I rush over to see the puppies.

They especially love Weston. He sits on the floor and gets literally dog-piled—the whole pack of fuzzy golden puppies tripping over his legs, licking his hands, and climbing into his lap. He laughs and pets them, and I sit back on my heels, watching—my heart swelling with cuteness overload.

There is something so unexplainably attractive about watching your boyfriend play with puppies. I snap a picture when he's not looking, but I know nothing can capture this feeling of love spilling over inside me.

"Which one is ours?" I ask, tickling a little fuzzy belly as it rolls over for me.

"I think she said we can choose," Weston says.

"That one really likes you." I giggle as the puppy in his lap starts licking his face.

He lifts it up to look underneath. "It's a boy, too."

I move closer, sitting next to Weston and scratching the puppy behind its velvety ears. "He looks like a Thor."

"Thor?"

"That's what Henry wants to name his dog," I explain with a self-satisfied smirk. "Bet you didn't even *think* to ask him that."

Weston laughs. "Nope. I didn't." He turns back to the puppy. "You want to come home with us, Thor?"

He yips excitedly and jumps up to kiss Weston again—tail wagging a mile a minute.

I grin. "That seems like a yes."

Bringing a puppy home is more difficult than bringing a baby home. At least, that's what Mrs. Ludovico says on the drive back to my house.

Thor sits in the backseat between Weston and me, looking up at me with those adorable brown eyes—it's impossible to resist cuddling him. Thankfully, he doesn't have any accidents on my dress, and Michelle provided me with a whole package of potty-training pads, to spare our floors any damage.

When we arrive back at my house, everything is a happy chaos of voices and laughter and coos of "Oh my goodness, he's so adorable!" directed at the puppy, not Weston—but I think they both deserve equal admiration for their cuteness.

Grandma has already partitioned off a play area for Thor in the living room, and we've decided to let him sleep in the laundry room, where he won't get into any mischief.

While Weston and I get the puppy settled in the living room, Mrs. Ludovico introduces herself to my mom and lavishes gratitude on my grandmother for her willingness to take care of the puppy until Christmas.

"I can never thank you enough," she says. "Henry will be so thrilled—oh, and I would love it if you all came over for Christmas Eve. If you don't have any other plans, that is."

"No, we don't," Grandma replies, sounding pleasantly surprised by the invitation. "But won't you be having family over?"

Mrs. Ludovico shakes her head. "No. All my family live out of state, and David's parents visited at Thanksgiving, so… it's just us. We like to keep it small, but you know—special. We'd love to have you all."

I smile, a little spark of excitement lighting up inside me as I overhear these plans being made. There is no other way I would like to spend Christmas Eve than with Weston and his family—even if Mom *is* there, it will be far better than staying home.

Maybe I'll even get a new dress for the occasion and surprise Weston.

"What's that smile for?" he asks, giving me a suspicious side-eye.

I shake my head and say, "Nothing."

Taking care of a puppy is exhausting. I spend the whole day fussing over him—feeding him, playing with him, cleaning up his various messes, and holding him while he sleeps. Good thing he's the cutest little ball of fluff that ever walked the earth, or I wouldn't be able to forgive him for demanding so much of my time.

I head to bed early, but end up on my computer, cluelessly scrolling Pinterest for gift ideas.

I still don't know what to get Weston for Christmas. His brothers' suggestions didn't help at all, and by this point I've run out of time to order something online—so my limited options are even *more* limited.

I feel like such a failure. I wanted to give him something special, something that only *I* could give him. At this point, I'm beginning to think "time together" is the only thing that falls into that category. I may not be able to wrap it up in sparkly paper with a bow, but I can make it something Weston will enjoy.

Scrolling back up to the search bar, I type in FUN WINTER DATE IDEAS.

I need all the help I can get.

Some promising lists pop up right away, and I skim the options—most of which we've already done together.

"'Go sledding… Visit a tree farm… Go skiing.' Ugh, no." I sigh, reading on. "'Go stargazing'—Mm, cute, but too cold… 'Go for a winter walk through the woods.' Weston would probably like that, but it's also too cold… 'Go to a hockey game.' Hmm, at least that wouldn't involve being outside…"

I pop open a new tab and start searching for hockey events nearby, when a knock comes from my ajar bedroom door. Mom pokes her head in. "You still awake?"

"Yeah," I murmur, turning back to my laptop.

Mom makes herself right at home—walking inside and plopping

down in my desk chair. "Your room is so pretty."

"Thanks."

She watches me browse the internet for a minute; then at last she speaks.

"I feel like I haven't seen you at all."

I shrug, ignoring the pang of guilt in my stomach. "Well, sorry. I've been busy."

"There's no need to be sorry," Mom says. "It's just that I have less than a week left here."

Thank God.

"Maybe we can do something together tomorrow," she offers.

I freeze, thinking fast. "Uh, I don't know if I can. That is… Weston and I have plans for tomorrow. After he gets out of school."

"Where are you going?"

"Uh… Millbrook Forest."

"Oh, I remember that place," Mom says. "Dad used to take me up there when I was little. It's pretty in the snow."

"Yeah, it is. He used to take me, too—for 'listening walks.' He said you could hear the voice of God in the wind and the birdsong… if you were quiet enough." I smile, remembering those times.

It's strange to think that Grandpa was a dad to both me and my mom. Granted, he was a better dad than my biological father could have been, but still.

He shouldn't have had to be.

"So, yeah," I say, refocusing. "Weston wants to take me up there tomorrow for a romantic walk through the woods, just the two of us." I add that last detail just in case she gets some crazy idea about inviting herself along.

"Well, maybe we can hang out when you get back," she says. "Or the day after tomorrow."

Unfortunately, I don't have any plans for Tuesday, yet—but I'm sure I'll think of something before the day arrives. For now, I nod passively and say, "Yeah, maybe."

I turn my attention back to the laptop, figuring this conversation is over. But Mom doesn't leave. Instead, she picks up the notebook on my desk and starts reading what I've written inside.

"What's this?"

I glance up, and my heart does a pole vault. "That's my secret notebook. Please don't read it—"

"'If fate hadn't brought us together, I would do it myself. I'd go to the ends of the earth to find you'…" Mom smiles. "I think I can guess who *this* is about."

My face flushes hot with a mixture of embarrassment and anger as I pull the notebook out of her hands. "Those poems are private."

"Has Weston read them?" Mom asks.

"No. Are you kidding?" A nervous laugh bursts past my lips. "He doesn't even know I write poems about him. I think I would die if he read them."

Mom raises her eyebrows. "Gosh. What did you write in them?"

I roll my eyes. "Nothing like *that*. Just, you know, my deepest thoughts and feelings. I would feel… vulnerable, sharing them with Weston."

Mom thinks about it for a moment. "Love makes all of us vulnerable."

I might appreciate the truth in that statement if I heard it from anyone else. But when Mom says it, a flinching and frustrated part of me wants to shoot back: *What do you know about being vulnerable?*

"Well," I say, grabbing my phone, "it's getting late, and I want to call Weston before I go to sleep. So… goodnight."

Mom hesitates, like she wants to say something else but doesn't have the words. Finally, she says goodnight and leaves the room.

I text Weston, hoping he doesn't have plans for tomorrow. Luckily for me, "Weston" and "plans" are antonymous words in the dictionary.

TESSA:
Hey
Want to go to Millbrook Forest tomorrow when you get out of school??

> **WESTON:**
> is this Tessa or did someone steal her phone

TESSA:
LOL
It's me!

> **WESTON:**
> u do realize Millbrook Forest is OUTSIDE

TESSA:
Yes obviously

> **WESTON:**
> But u want to go?

TESSA:
yesss I want to go
with you
It will be pretty and romantic in the snow <3

WESTON:
u will be pretty in the snow ;)
Just make sure you wear a jacket this time so u don't
steal mine

TESSA:
Aw I like stealing ur things

WESTON:
yeah i noticed
First u steal my heart
Now my clothes
ur a thief

TESSA:
Yep. Sorry.

WESTON:
Don't be
I love it

TESSA:
Hey random but how much do you like hockey?
On a scale of 1 to 10

WESTON:
idk
8
I like it
But I'm not the guy who paints his face and screams at
the other team

TESSA:

Thank God

> **WESTON:**
> Why do you ask?

TESSA:

No reason

I mean there is a reason but

I'll tell you tomorrow ;)

If fate hadn't brought us together

I would do it myself

I'd go to the ends of the earth

to find you

to steal your heart

(thief that I am)

and give you my heart in return

and you'd say, "that's not mine."

and I'd say, "why don't you open it up and see?"

So you would look inside

(to prove me wrong)

but you wouldn't be able to

Because all you would find in my heart

is you.

WESTON

DECEMBER 20

TESSA IS ALL SMILES WHEN SHE COMES RACING OUT HER front door on Monday afternoon. I don't even have a chance to park my mom's car in her driveway—I blink, and Tessa is already in the passenger seat, diving over the center console to kiss me.

"You'll never guess what I got for us," she gasps, out of breath from her race to the car. "The *last* two seats—together, anyway—for the hockey game in Windsor Falls tomorrow. Oh, gosh, I can't remember the team names anymore... But I thought it would be fun to go together and make, like, a date of it."

I stare at her, stunned. "Are you sure you're the same Tessa?"

She blinks, disappointed at my reaction. "I thought you said you liked hockey."

"No, I do—that sounds great. I'm just... surprised." I laugh under my breath. "It doesn't seem like your speed."

Tessa grabs my hand and locks her fingers through mine. "My speed is your speed. Besides, I like trying new things."

I grin, pulling out onto the street. "Like wandering through the woods."

"I've been in the woods before," Tessa snaps, all defensive.

"Mm. I bet the last time you went, you were probably… twelve."

She tilts her head. "More like ten."

We both laugh, and I lift her hand to kiss her knuckles. I think it's cute that she went out of her way to get those tickets for us—even though she's the last person I would expect to get excited about hockey.

The radio plays some modern country hits station, and I sing along to the love songs because it makes Tessa smile in a way that lights up her eyes—and I could watch that happen all day, forever. She's enjoying it until halfway through "Body Like a Back Road" when she scrunches her eyebrows and says, "What is this song about?" And I burst out laughing.

When we arrive at Millbrook, the parking lot is fairly empty—and the trails are even less occupied. It's not too cold today, but cold enough for a flurry of snow. Tessa calls it "Hollywood snow" because it looks just like the fake snow you see in movies.

The woods are already covered in a few inches of powder, making everything seem frozen in time—literally. It's so quiet; the only sound to be heard is the crunching of our boots in the snow.

"Do you know where this trail goes?" Tessa asks, craning her neck to see what's ahead.

"I think it goes up past the horse farm and to some lookout. I don't know; it's been a while since I came here."

Tessa's funny—we literally *just* got here, and she already looks like she wants to go back. She's staring at the trail ahead like it's the start of an Everest expedition, not a gentle upward slope through wooded farmland.

About a half mile up the trail, we come to a clearing that opens up to the farm. Two horses glance up at us from behind a split-rail fence—tails swishing, noses puffing clouds of steam in the cold. Tessa runs over to pet them, and I take pictures of her when she's not looking.

"Should we head back now?" she says when the horses return to eating their hay.

"Uh, we just started."

"We've been hiking for *miles*."

I stifle a laugh. "That was, like... less than one mile, Tes."

She sighs.

"Come on. Let's just go a little further."

"*Farther*," she corrects like a smart-ass, trudging into step beside me.

We hike *farther* up the trail, through the snowy woods, in the direction of where the lookout was marked on the map back in the parking lot. But after about ten minutes of walking, I start to wonder why we haven't seen a single person on this trail. And why the trail seems to be getting narrower and narrower.

Tessa stops, huffing and puffing, turning in a slow circle as she studies the woods around us. "Are we lost?"

"No, we're not *lost*," I argue, trying to sound confident. "We're just on an unmarked trail."

"That's not funny."

"I didn't say it was funny."

"You're laughing."

I guess I am. And now Tessa is glaring at me like she *really* wants to go back.

"Oh, god," she groans. "It's going to be dark soon—"

"Hey, don't panic. We're going to find the trail, okay? And even if we don't—"

Tessa smacks my arm. "Don't say that!"

"Even if we *don't*, we'll survive. We can make a fire and build a shelter in the woods and sleep under the stars and huddle together for warmth..." I pull her into a bear hug to illustrate.

She whimpers and buries her face in my chest. "I'm not sleeping in the woods!" she wails, her voice muffled by my jacket.

I grin, rubbing her back. "I thought you liked trying new things."

She tips her chin up to glare at me. "Thanks a lot."

"Hey, you're the one who wanted to come here."

"I *knowww*, because I thought it would be romantic. I didn't think you would get us *lost*."

"What could be more romantic than getting lost in the woods together?"

She grunts. "There's nothing romantic about this."

"Oh yeah?" I say, taking that as a challenge. "I'm sure I can think of a way to make it more romantic..." My gaze drifts over Tessa's face, resting on her lips. A little smile starts to form there, but I don't see much of it before I lean in and kiss her.

She melts, as usual—her arms looping around my neck as she kisses me back, forgetting all about being lost in the woods.

Mission accomplished.

A breathless laugh spills out of her mouth and into mine. "You're just trying to distract me, aren't you?"

"No," I whisper against her neck, hiding a smirk in her hair. "I think *you're* the one getting distracted."

"Oh, shut up." She giggles. "You're the one kissing me."

"You're the one kissing *me*."

"I'm not kissing you."

I touch my lips to hers again, softly. "Liar."

An annoyed spark lights up her eyes, and she smashes our faces together, angry-kissing me like she never has before. It catches me off guard, but feels pretty awesome. Until I stumble backwards, trip on a root, and fall on my ass.

Tessa comes crashing down on top of me, and then we're both lying in the snow, laughing uncontrollably.

"Wow—good thing your grandparents didn't see that. I don't think they'd let me go places alone with you… for my own safety."

Tessa rolls her eyes, but she's still laughing. Then she stops suddenly and goes, "Shh. Did you hear that?"

"Hear what?"

We both fall silent and listen for a long moment. First there is nothing—then the sound comes again. Voices, distant and drifting through the trees.

"Damn," I mutter, shutting my eyes. "Looks like we won't be having that romantic campout after all."

"Another time, perhaps."

We cut through the forest, following the sound of the strangers' voices until we spill out onto the main trail, which is more like a narrow dirt road. Just around the corner, we find the lookout—a panoramic view of the snow-dusted mountains rolling in every direction.

"It's so beautiful," Tessa breathes, her words a puff of steam. Snowflakes catch in her hair and melt against her flushed cheeks.

I circle my arm around her waist, and she points out something about the valley yawning below us, but I don't really pay attention— I'm too busy noticing how beautiful *she* is.

It's dusk by the time we get back to the parking lot. Tessa's fingers are like icicles, so we spend a few minutes sitting in the car—me breathing into her hands and her laughing about how she really thought we might have to spend the night in the woods.

When we get back on the road, I assume I'm heading to her house, but about halfway there she says, "We can't go home yet."

"Why not?"

Tessa stares at the dashboard clock, looking apprehensive. "Because…"

I wait, raising one eyebrow.

"Because it's so boring there."

"I thought you liked staying home."

"Well, I do, but…" Tessa looks away, and for a moment she wordlessly draws lines through the fog on her window.

I'm starting to worry about what the rest of the sentence might be.

But I'm trying to avoid my mom?

She huffs a sigh, turning to face me. "But I'm trying to be more adventurous. Like you."

She sounds sincere enough that I don't doubt her. It's actually kind of cute, because her attempts at being adventurous are anything but. I know she hated ninety percent of that "romantic woodland hike"—yet she kept a smile on her face, for my sake.

"Let's go get something to eat," she says. "I'm starving. What about you?"

"I'm always starving."

And that's how we end up at a diner downtown, stuffing our faces with fries and milkshakes. Tessa seems to forget all about the time—and the rest of the world, for that matter. I love this spontaneous girl sitting across from me, but I can't help thinking there's more to her sudden thirst for "adventure."

Is she doing all this for my sake?

I finally come right out and ask her.

And she stares at me like she's been caught doing something wrong. "Well, yeah, I guess…" She glances down at the table.

I study that expression, knowing her well enough to see that she's hiding something. But I keep my mouth shut, waiting for her to spill it on her own.

"I know how boring I can be," she murmurs, playing with the straw in her milkshake. "I like to just stay home and bake cookies and watch movies and cuddle you."

I shrug. "I like that, too."

"Yeah, but it's not your favorite thing. You like exciting stuff, and I just… I'm not as fun and adventurous as you are."

I grin, reaching over and taking her hand. "Tessa, I love you exactly as you are. Don't feel like you have to change a single thing about you, or… be more like me."

Her eyes soften, and she smiles a little.

"Trust me, if you were boring, I would tell you. In fact, I wouldn't have to tell you because I wouldn't be dating you."

She collapses into giggles.

"I'm serious," I say. "You're the wildest roller-coaster ride of a girl I've ever met. Why do you think I fell in love with you?"

"But nobody else thinks I'm wild," Tessa argues.

"Then nobody knows you like I do."

She squeezes my hand and whispers, "No, they don't." But even now, I can see a shadow of something in her eyes—regret or guilt; I'm not sure what.

"Do you still want to go to the game tomorrow?" I ask.

"Yes, of course!" she says, without a second's hesitation. "It was so hard to get those tickets. And it's not outside, so… I'm sure it will be fun."

We both look at each other for a moment, then burst out laughing.

❄ ❄ ❄

Later that night, I'm trying to get through the mountain of homework that's been accumulating on my desk over the past few days—but I can't concentrate. All I can think about is Tessa.

All the things we've done together.

All the things I want us to do together.

All the times I've made her smile or laugh. How I wish she were here right now so I could hear her laugh.

She looked so beautiful today, petting the horses, kissing me in the woods. I loved the way her eyes lit up when she first jumped in the car and told me about the hockey game—how she was all excited to surprise me.

Now it gets me thinking: I should surprise *her* with something tomorrow. Something more her speed.

Especially since I *still* don't know what the hell I'm getting her for Christmas. The least I can do is make tomorrow's date something special for her. I'll definitely take her out to dinner before the game, but what else can I surprise her with?

She doesn't really dig surprises, so I have to make sure it's a safe bet that I won't have to worry about. But not too safe that it's boring.

The last thing I want to be is boring.

I find my phone buried in a grave of homework and send Tessa a text.

WESTON:

Hey beautiful

I'm picking u up at 4 ok?

> **TESSA:**
>
> Hey handsome
>
> 4pm tomorrow?

WESTON:

No

4 in the morning

We gonna bust u outta there and go PARTY

> **TESSA:**
>
> ur so silly
>
> Yes 4pm is good
>
> But won't we be like 2 hours early??

WESTON:

Dude I'm taking you out to dinner first

> **TESSA:**
>
> Dude?

WESTON:

*love

*darling

*goDDESS DIVINE

TESSA:
That's more like it ;)
Where are you taking me?

I have no idea. I haven't thought that far ahead. I just assumed that we would figure it out when we got there, but now Tessa is making me feel kind of lame for not having something already planned and reserved for us.

That's what smart boyfriends do, right?

WESTON:
guess

TESSA:
Hmmm
The Old Stone Inn?

WESTON:
YEP

TESSA:
omg really? I love that place!
It's so cozy and romantic

I can't help but laugh, because that was pretty damn smooth. I write a note to myself to make reservations for the Old Stone Inn tomorrow.

So that's dinner taken care of... but what about the Surprise Thing?

I want to take her somewhere special—give her a perfect date. Show her that I love her for exactly who she is, because I do. I wouldn't change a single thing about her.

I only hope she feels the same way about me.

TESSA

DECEMBER 21

"*THERE SHE IS,*" *MOM SAYS WHEN I SHUFFLE INTO THE* kitchen wearing pajama pants and Weston's hoodie, my hair in a messy bun.

I cup my hand over a yawn. "Good morning."

I've slept preposterously late, but I don't mind. Perks of being homeschooled. Breakfast has come and gone, but Grandma has kept some French toast warm in the skillet for me. When I take a seat at the table, Mom turns to me and says, "I was hoping to snatch you before you start your day."

"Oh?" I raise an eyebrow cautiously, drizzling maple syrup over my toast. "Why? What's up?"

Grandma gives me a chiding look, as though I should inherently *know* what's up. "Your mom was just telling me how she wants to spend some time with you today."

"I was thinking we could go out later," Mom suggests with a keen smile. "You know, just the two of us. Do some Christmas shopping, maybe grab something to eat. You can show me some of your favorite places."

She looks so genuinely eager to please, I almost feel bad refusing this time. But even if I *wanted* to go out with her, I couldn't.

"Oh, I'm so sorry," I say, with all the remorse I can muster. "I forgot to mention… Weston and I made plans to go to this hockey game in Windsor Falls."

As the words come out of my mouth, I realize how they make me sound: like I'm doing this on purpose—evading my mother with any excuse I can find. Thinking fast, I add, "Weston surprised me with it yesterday, last minute. It's all arranged now."

Grandma frowns at me critically. "Can't you disarrange it? Your mother is only here for a few more days."

"No," I argue, my body stiffening. "I can't *disarrange* it. Weston was so looking forward to going with me… He said it was really hard to get the tickets. I would hate to disappoint him."

I feel a bit unscrupulous for lying about the tickets, but it's just a harmless little fib—for everyone's good. I don't want to explain my reasoning, or apologize for wanting to go on a date with my boyfriend. I shouldn't have to.

As I suspected, nobody has a problem with my plans when they think it was *Weston's* idea. Mom just pushes a discontented smile onto her face and says, "That's okay. I understand. You guys want to be together."

Grandma still looks disappointed in me, but what does she expect? That I'll forfeit precious time with Weston to have an awkward mother-daughter shopping trip?

She clearly doesn't know me at all.

In fact, I'm beginning to feel like Weston is the only one who truly gets me.

"What time are you leaving?" Mom asks.

"Weston's picking me up at four."

"Oh. Well, maybe we can do something before then."

I poke at my French toast with a fork. "Maybe. I have some blog work I need to catch up on first. I slept so late…"

Grandma fixes her gaze firmly on mine. "I'd like for you to stay home tomorrow. No more all-day excursions. I need someone to look after that little rascal," she says, gesturing towards Thor, who is chasing his tail around the kitchen.

My heart sinks, not because of my responsibility to take care of the sweet little puppy—but because I know Grandma's *real* reason for keeping me home: to force mother-daughter time down my throat.

"Alright," I relent, hiding my displeasure behind a forced smile. "If that's what you want."

Grandma gives a decided nod. "It is."

❄ ❄ ❄

I finish my school and blog work early, but I don't spend my free hour with Mom—instead, I take extra time to get ready for my date. First, I do my makeup and curl my hair, then I spend a good twenty minutes deliberating over the perfect outfit—something classy enough for the Old Stone Inn but casual enough for a hockey game. I decide on a blush sweater tucked into a pink-and-gray plaid skater skirt (with leggings underneath for extra warmth) and heeled booties to match. Last but not least, I gloss my lips and spritz myself with that sugarplum perfume Weston likes so much.

He pulls into the driveway at quarter to four, and I dash outside before he can get any ideas about coming in the house.

"Ooh, you bribed your dad into lending you his truck?"

Weston laughs, shutting the driver's door behind him. "No bribing necessary." He grins, his eyes lighting up as he takes me in. "Wow. You look like a million bucks."

I smile, my heart fluttering. "So do you," I whisper, lifting up on my tiptoes to kiss his cheek.

"Pfft. You just say that to make me feel better."

"I do *not*."

"It's okay." He winks, opening the passenger door for me. "I like having the prettiest girl in the world on my arm. Makes everyone wish they were me. And that's something that doesn't usually happen."

I giggle, my face blushing as pink as my sweater.

Once we're driving, I pull out my phone and ask Weston what music I should put on. He tells me he doesn't care; then he smirks and says, "I made a playlist for you. *About* you, I mean."

"What?" My heart nearly explodes. "Oh my gosh. I love you so much."

"You haven't even heard it yet. It could just be 'Body Like a Back Road' fifty times in a row."

"If it is, I'm going to smack you."

I steal Weston's phone and find the playlist right away—it's titled "Tessa," with a yellow heart emoji next to it, and just seeing that makes me swoon and want to kiss him.

The playlist is perfect—a mixtape of The Lumineers, Sleeping At Last, Billy Raffoul, and The Mowgli's. Mostly songs I've introduced him to, but a few I've never heard before that he says remind him of me.

A lot of thought goes into a good playlist. You have to build the mood, slowly and surely. It's like a road trip, actually. Slowly transitioning from one feeling to the next. Weston is surprisingly good at curating playlists. I tell him that, and he says, "Surprisingly?" with an offended little laugh.

I could fall in love with the way his hands rest on the wheel. I watch them in the golden sunlight as it etches the veins in his forearms. He's wearing a white button-down shirt with the sleeves rolled halfway up, and there's something extremely attractive about it. Our hands are laced together over the cupholders, and I think that's the part I fall in love with the most—knowing that he belongs to me and I belong to him. I don't think there's a more beautiful feeling than that in all the world.

I catch him smirking and say, "What are you thinking about?"

"I can't tell you," he replies. "Not yet, anyway. It's a surprise."

"A surprise?"

"For tonight. I'm taking you somewhere after the game."

"Oh?" I feel my eyebrows rise. "You never said."

"That's because it's a *surprise.*"

"I'm not too good with surprises, Wes…"

He laughs. "You'll like this one. I promise."

I decide to trust him. I sit back and hold his hand and watch the line on my GPS get shorter and shorter as we near Windsor Falls.

The sun has set by the time we pull into the parking lot of the Old Stone Inn. Weston's hand slides into mine as we walk in together. I smile up at him, my boots clicking on the stone steps. I love this place: the white tablecloths and flickering candles and the massive sparkling Christmas tree standing by a tall stone fireplace.

I remember coming here with Grandma and Grandpa when I was younger. Never did I imagine I would be sitting at one of these cozy tables for two, looking over at my *boyfriend* in the romantic candle-light.

All through dinner, I try to make him tell me about this "surprise" he has planned for later. But he refuses to spoil it.

"And don't go imagining what it could be, either. It might not be as great as you think. And I know how you are with failed expectations."

I roll my eyes, but he's right. It's one of my weaknesses—getting my hopes up, only to have them dashed one way or another. So, although I'm dying of curiosity, I stop trying to guess.

Instead, I live in the moment. Somehow, that's so much easier to do with a cute boyfriend who buys me dinner and stares at me with a moonstruck light in his eyes. I feel like a million bucks when he looks at me like that.

It's six by the time we leave the restaurant, so we head straight for the Civic Center, which is now called something else and nearly impossible to find on my navigation. But Weston finds it, and then we're dashing through the parking lot, our laughter making puffs of steam in the cold.

It's not nearly as cold inside the rink despite the giant slab of ice glistening under the lights. Loud rock music pumps from the speakers overhead as we wander around trying to find our seats. We sit there forever before the game actually begins—and even then, I'm not sure what is going on. I've never been able to make much sense of sports, so I have to ask Weston for commentary on which team is doing better than the other.

It's all loud and chaotic and totally *not* my speed. Weston was right, and he takes the opportunity to rub my nose in it.

"See? I know you better than you know yourself."

I shove him. "Oh, shut up. I'm having fun."

"That must be why you keep checking the time," he says, with a little know-it-all smirk.

When the second intermission thing happens, I sneak off to find the bathroom. It takes forever to weave through the crowd of people, and by the time I return to our seats, the players are back to body-slamming each other, and Weston is eating some kind of very unhealthy-looking food.

"What is that?"

"Chili cheese fries," he says. "Want some?"

"No. We just ate. How can you still be hungry?"

What I really want to know is how he can put away all this food and still have shredded abs. It's not fair. I flop down in my seat, checking the time again—only twenty minutes left to this game, thank God.

Weston seems to be enjoying it, though, and I'm happy as long as *he's* happy—but I'm even happier when the home team wins and the game is over. I practically drag Weston outside, "To get ahead of the crowd," I tell him—but he laughs because he can read my mind better than that.

The night sky is clear and sparkling with stars as we cut back through the parking lot.

"Time for my surprise?" I say, looking expectantly at Weston.

His smile betrays him. "Mm-hmm."

We drive downtown, and I watch the storefronts roll past—their windows lit up gold, making the snow-crested sidewalk shimmer. The village looks so magical and festive, dressed up in twinkle lights and evergreen boughs.

Weston parallel parks the truck (a feat in itself), and we get out, walking halfway down the block before he stops in front of a shop and turns to me.

"I think this is it."

I take one look in the windows, and my jaw drops.

It's the most adorable bookstore I've ever seen. A sign over the door reads "Bell & Brontë" in swirly vintage lettering, and the whole storefront looks like something from the 1930s—warm lamplight slipping through tall bookshelves to beckon us inside. Speechless, I grab Weston's hand and pull him through the door.

It's even cozier than it looks—the aroma of coffee and pastries greets me along with the soft Christmas music playing from another room. The whole shop is set up more like a library: little reading nooks tucked between the shelves, plump leather chairs draped with blankets and flickering in the light of the fireplace that crackles invitingly at one side of the room.

"This place is so adorable," I gush to Weston, who is watching my reaction like it's the highlight of his night. "How did you find it?"

He grins. "Online. After about two hours of trying to figure out where to take you."

"Oh my gosh, you didn't have to do all that."

"I wanted to," he says, hugging me from behind. "I wanted you to know that I appreciate you. And how you went out of your way to do something you knew I would like. I wanted to surprise you with something I knew *you* would like."

My heart swells with love for him—but I also feel a pang of guilt in the pit of my stomach, because he's not entirely right about that. I didn't plan this date just because I knew he would like it.

For the second time today, I feel deceitful. And it's even worse now, because Weston is so sweet and unsuspecting. While I was scheming ways to evade my mother, he was losing sleep thinking of a way to make tonight more enjoyable for me.

I don't deserve him.

But I fully intend to savor my time with him now that I'm here. After all, this will be our last "all-day excursion" for a while. So I push my shameful feelings to the back of my mind and explore the bookstore with Weston.

We wander through the chaos of books and find a cafe at the back of the store—the source of the amazing smells I noticed before. Weston buys us hot chocolate, and we drift around through the maze of bookshelves, hand in hand.

"Remember our first bookstore date?" I say.

Weston laughs under his breath. "How could I forget? I almost committed murder."

"Pfft. You wouldn't have. That boy was just being a jerk."

Weston gives me a look, like *come on.* "He was *assaulting* you. Let's just say it's a good thing you weren't my girlfriend at the time. Or else I would have made him wish he'd never been born."

I bite down on a smile, flattered to be so aggressively protected. "You did *call* me your girl, though."

"I did?"

"Mm-hmm. I remember it was the first time you ever said anything like that, and I was all at sea the next day because of it."

Weston frowns at me with a little amused glint in his eyes. "Really?"

I nod. "That was when I first started to realize that I had a crush on you. Of course, it took me much longer to admit it—even to myself." I look down at our hands laced together and gently stroke my thumb over his knuckles. "And now I can't imagine my life without you."

When I look back up into his eyes, I find him studying me with an expression so soft and almost surprised, it's as if I've just unveiled a new side of myself that he's never seen before. "Do you really mean that?" he says, breaking my heart a little with how unconvinced he sounds.

"Of course I mean it. I love you, Weston."

"I know… But what does love mean to you?"

This seems strangely philosophical and out of the blue for Weston, but I think seriously about my answer before replying.

"Well… it means wanting to be with the person you love all the time. And when you're not with them, you're thinking about them. About all the ways they make your life brighter… and so much more beautiful." I smile, lowering my voice as I pull him closer. "Love means never wanting to leave their side. And dreaming about the days when you won't have to."

Weston turns to give me a look, caught a little off guard—that adorable smirk twitching at his lips. "You mean the *future* future?"

I giggle, hiding a blush behind my hair. "Mm-hmm."

"Well," he says, stopping as we reach a secluded corner of the bookshop, "based on those symptoms, it would seem I'm just as lovesick as you are." He grins, leaning close to my ear and whispering, "Is it serious?"

"Mm-hmm." I reach up to trace my finger along his jaw. "Incurable. I hear some people have even died from it."

"Oh yeah?" he murmurs, his eyes darting back and forth between mine. "Well, I've cheated death before."

I breathe a laugh, then pull him down to my level to kiss him slowly—leaning back against the bookshelves and losing my fingers in his hair. For a moment, I forget where we are. There is nothing but the heavy warmth of Weston's hand on my waist, his lips moving softly over mine, his spicy scent filling my lungs and drawing me in like a spell.

I could go on kissing him forever, but I force myself to ease back—before someone catches us.

"Wow," he whispers. "I should take you to bookstores more often."

A little breathless laugh spills past my lips. "We have to buy something before we leave. Oh, you know what we should do?"

"What? Make out some more?" He pulls me closer.

"No." I giggle, pressing a finger to his lips before they can take mine captive again. "We should buy a book for each other. You can pick out something that I would like, and I'll pick out something that you would like."

He grunts. "Good luck. I don't read. Unless I'm forced to."

"Well, I bet I could find a book that even *you* would like." I smile. "Oh, let's do it! Come on, it'll be fun. And how about we get the books gift-wrapped, and I won't open mine until I'm alone in my room tonight—and you won't open yours until you're alone, too."

Weston frowns. "Why?"

"Because. It's more romantic that way. We can text each other as we unwrap them."

"Alright."

The challenge is on. We part ways, wandering to different sections of the bookstore. I go straight to nonfiction, because there's no way Weston will read a novel. After a few minutes of scanning the books, my gaze falls to a shelf labeled "Happiness." If ever there were a genre for Weston, this is it.

I run my fingertip over the titles, recognizing some of them. A particularly thin one catches my attention. I pull it out and instantly remember the cover.

Perfect.

Hiding the book behind my back, I retrace my steps to the front of the store where I spotted the checkout earlier. Weston is already there, paying for my book. Gosh, he's fast.

I watch from a distance as he takes a pen from the cashier and writes something on the inside leaf of the book.

That's a great idea.

I duck behind a bookshelf and excavate a pen from my purse, opening the book in my hands and writing an inscription inside.

To my sweet Weston...

WESTON

DECEMBER 21

WE SWAP BOOKS AS SOON AS WE'RE BACK IN THE TRUCK.
They're both gift-wrapped in old-fashioned Christmas paper, so I have
no idea what Tessa picked for me, and she has no idea what I picked
for her. But her eyes light up with a smile as I place it in her hands.

"Now, this isn't my Christmas gift to you," I say.

"Oh?" Tessa raises an eyebrow. "So you figured out the other
one?"

I clear my throat nervously, nodding. "Uh, yeah. All figured out."

It's not all figured out. It's not even a little bit figured out.

"I have *your* gift all figured out, too," Tessa says. But there's a
strain of hesitation in her voice. I wonder if we're both lying.

It's almost ten, and Tessa has a curfew of eleven, so we start
driving back. I don't want to play it too close.

Tessa whines, "We have *plenty* of time," which is kind of weird
for her. She's usually the early bird—but I guess it's like she told me in
the bookstore: you want to be with the person you love all the time.

It's still sinking in. The way she looked at me, her eyes glittering in the firelight. The way she kissed me and ran her fingers through my hair. The way she said, "I love you, Weston."

I'm starting to believe it.

I'm starting to trust that this is real. This is mine.

She is mine.

What more proof do I need? After tonight, I would be a moron to doubt her.

She doesn't wish things were different.

She doesn't wish *I* were different.

She loves me.

All of this hits me at once, and it's an emotion I've never felt before. Tessa's hand is woven through mine, and love songs are playing softly from the radio as we drive through the dark, but I don't feel like I'm driving—I feel like I'm flying. Like I'm floating off the ground. Like I have fireworks going off in my chest.

Maybe it's not anything new—maybe I've felt like this all along, but I just couldn't tell because I let the voices of doubt in my head win. I let them beat me, back me into the corner, push me right out of the damn ring.

I was too scared to fight back. But now I can see that those voices were just smoke and mirrors. Lies. They're gone now—and I can barely remember what they told me. Like a bunch of crap you have to memorize for a test, but you forget it afterwards because it no longer matters.

Suddenly nothing matters except us.

When we get back into Rockford, Tessa has me take the long route, down Main Street. "Drive slow," she says, "so we can see the Christmas lights."

I smile, bringing her hand up to kiss her knuckles. "Your wish is my command."

I drive slowly down Main Street, and Tessa looks out at the lights and says something about how pretty our town looks right now, but all I can think about is how pretty *she* looks right now—her curls spilling down the side of her neck, her eyes sparkling in the colorful light.

We make it home with ten minutes to spare. The lights are still on in the living room, so Tessa says, "Why don't you come inside and say hi to Thor?"

I grin. "And your grandparents?"

"Yeah, them too."

But when we get inside, Tessa's grandparents aren't around. Only her mom is. She looks up from the couch, where she's watching some reality TV show on low volume.

"Where's Grandma?" is the first thing out of Tessa's mouth.

"Oh, they went to bed. I told them I'd stay up and make sure you got home safe."

I can feel Tessa tense up at that, and I see a flicker of irritation flash through her eyes. "Well, you didn't have to," she mutters, going into the next room to find Thor.

Heather opens her mouth to reply, but Tessa's already gone. She turns to me with an exasperated laugh. "Hi, Weston. How was the game?"

"It was good," I say. "Not really Tessa's thing, but I took her to this hipster bookstore afterwards, so… I think the night was a success."

"Aw, I'm glad you guys had a good time. I heard it was really hard for you to get those tickets, so last minute."

I shake my head. "Oh, I didn't get the tickets. Tessa did. She surprised me with them yesterday."

Heather frowns, puzzled. "Really? She told me that *you* surprised *her*."

What the heck? Why would Tessa lie about that? She was so excited to tell me about it yesterday, so proud that she was able to snag the last two seats together.

Why would she make her mom think the whole thing was *my* idea?

So she wouldn't feel bad for staying out all day?

Suspicion creeps up on me like a dark cloud, throwing a cold shadow over the way I felt just moments ago.

Was she using me as an excuse?

That's when Tessa comes back into the room, cooing over the puppy in her arms. Thor starts squirming excitedly when he sees me, and Tessa laughs—but I can't think straight. I'm still stuck on what her mom said. And on the feeling of dread sinking into my stomach.

I absentmindedly scratch Thor behind the ears, wondering if I should just go home and not ask Tessa about it. Leave things on a good note. But if I do that, I know I'll be up all night trying to figure it out. Wondering if it was *all* just smoke and mirrors. Lies.

No.

I need to know the truth.

"Tessa," I say softly, meeting her gaze, "can I talk to you for a minute? Outside?"

She quirks one eyebrow. "Outside?"

"I can leave," Heather offers.

"No, you're fine," I say, handing her the puppy. "Keep an eye on Thor for a minute. We'll be right back."

Tessa studies me, clueless. She can see that something is wrong, that I'm not just taking her outside to kiss her and whisper sweet nothings in her ear.

I wish I were.

Tessa follows me out into the cold night, shutting the front door behind her. "Is something wrong?" she asks, her voice small and uneasy.

I walk halfway to the curb, making sure we're well out of earshot before speaking. "Why did you tell your mom that I got the tickets?"

Tessa freezes, guilt written all over her face. It's enough to prove my suspicions right—but I need to hear her say it.

"Your mom just told me that you said I was the one who got the tickets... And that it was *my* idea to go to the game. Is that true?"

Tessa swallows. "Yes... I did. But there wasn't anything devious about it. I just wanted to have a fun date with you and not have to apologize for it."

A flare of anger rises in my chest. "So you used me. As an excuse."

"Weston—"

"Did you actually *want* to do any of that stuff with me? Or were you just trying to avoid your mom? Just trying to stay out as late as possible so you wouldn't have to see her—not because you want to be with me." My voice wavers at the end, and it makes me feel like a pansyass, but those words will burn me if I keep them inside.

Tessa looks shocked. "I *do* want to be with you—"

"Then why did you lie to your mother?"

"Because. I knew that if I told her it was my idea, she would think I was just... trying to avoid her on purpose—"

"And would she be wrong?"

Tessa gapes at me for a long moment. Speechless.

"Isn't that the *real* reason you got the tickets, Tessa? Planned this whole date? Isn't that the real reason you wanted to go to Millbrook yesterday?" I mutter a humorless laugh, because I can't believe I was too stupid to see all of this for what it was. "I thought you were going out of your way to be with me. Now I see that you were just going out of your way to *not* be with *her*."

"That's not true!" Tessa bursts out. "You've got it all wrong."

"Really?"

"Yes. It wasn't like that. I *did* want to be with you. But…"

I stiffen. "But?"

She works her jaw, a fire burning in her eyes along with a thousand words she doesn't speak. Finally, she looks away, sighing dramatically. "You wouldn't understand, Weston—"

"Try me." My voice is as hard as steel. I'm holding her feet to the fire on this one. Whether she likes it or not.

Spoiler: she does *not*.

She takes a step closer to me, her voice low and bitter. "You have no idea how exhausting it's been having her here."

I almost laugh. "Exhausting?"

"Yes. She's constantly pestering me to spend time with her… She acts like there's nothing wrong."

"And what *is* wrong?"

She squints at me like I've lost my memory. "*Everything*. Don't you remember what I told you?"

"I remember you saying that people don't change. That your mother never sacrificed anything for you and that's why you can't forgive her—"

"She never *asked* for my forgiveness," Tessa argues. "She just showed up here out of nowhere, thinking we could forget the past and be one big happy family. But where was she all this time? Where was she after the accident? When I needed a mother the most, she wasn't there. She never has been. She never calls me, all year—"

"The phone works both ways, you know."

Tessa's eyebrows shoot up. "Excuse me?"

"How many times did you call her, all those years?" I say, turning the tables. "How many times did you try to fix the problem yourself?"

Tessa scoffs. "How could I have 'fixed the problem'? I was a child."

"So?"

"So it's not my responsibility! I shouldn't have to be the one to call her and try to keep a relationship going."

"Shouldn't have to?" I spit back. "Just like I shouldn't have to put up with people staring at me because I'm missing limbs? Welcome to the real world, Tessa—where we do shit that we shouldn't have to do!"

She bristles, startled by my anger.

I know I should lay off at this point, but it's not happening—my temper has broken its chains. I get right in her face, lowering my voice. "I live every day of my life doing stuff I shouldn't have to do. But I don't sit around complaining about how I wish I didn't have to do it— I *have* to. Yeah, it sucks. But that's just the way things are. So maybe you should stop looking around for someone to point the finger at... and instead take a look in the mirror and see what *you* can do about it."

Maybe that was a little harsh, but I can't sugarcoat the truth. I don't know how.

Tessa stares at me, her eyes flashing—brimming with tears. Our breath clouds in the cold, swirling violently between us. There's a long, tense moment of silence.

Then Tessa speaks, her voice like ice. "How dare you—"

"How dare I? How dare *you* hide behind me and act like *I'm* the one keeping you away from your mother when all I want is for you to make things right with her and be happy—"

"Oh, really?" Tessa sputters, tears quivering in her eyes. "You want me to be happy? As you *bully* me—"

144

"I'm not bullying you," I seethe, my jaw clenching. "I'm being honest. Sorry if you can't handle it, but I'm not gonna lie just to make you feel better." I try to hold back, but there's a knife in my chest, and it hurts like hell, and I want her to feel it too. I lower my voice and say, "I'm not as good a liar as *you* are."

That cuts. I see the pain flash through her eyes, and I immediately want to take my words back, but I can't. I've struck a match and thrown it into a pool of gasoline, and now?

She explodes.

"How dare you! I've done *nothing* wrong—yet here you are, crucifying me like you have the *right to*? Well, you don't! And I won't put up with it." Tessa takes a step closer, her voice trembling. "You know what I *hate* about you, Weston?"

That feels like a kick in the gut.

But I absorb the pain, shoving it down. I'm pissed now—locked up and ready to take her shots.

"What?" I mock, egging her on. "What is it you hate about me?"

"I hate how you *always* think you're right, a hundred percent of the time!" Tessa rages, her eyes ablaze. "You're so arrogant, so... rude and offensive. You always have been! If I'm dealing with a problem, you just go ahead and make it *your* problem. You're always pushing in where you're not wanted, always bossing me around like you know best. It's insufferable! *You're* insufferable!" She shoves me hard, and I stagger back a step. "You just don't know when to *shut up*, do you?"

I stare at her, wordless. I thought I was ready to hear all that—to stand here and take it like a man. But now I feel like I have a hundred knives stuck in me. And God almighty, it hurts.

It hurts because I see the look in Tessa's eyes.

She means it.

Every word.

She's the one being honest now.

And I'm the one who can't handle it.

"Tessa—"

"Don't." She cuts me off, her breath ragged. "Don't say another word." And with that, she turns away—storming back into the house and slamming the door behind her.

For a long moment I stand frozen in place, staring at the door. My heart thundering, breaking, bleeding in my chest.

My world burning down around me.

And there's nothing I can do.

TESSA

DECEMBER 21

I'M UP ALL NIGHT.

Crying.

My bedroom door is locked, and my pillow is soaked with tears—I've been using it to muffle my sobs so that my grandparents won't hear me crying. Mom caught sight of my tears when I first ran into the house, but I didn't stop to explain what was wrong. I just ran straight to my room and shut the door.

For hours, I lie in the dark on my rumpled bed and cry until I have no tears left in me.

How could Weston say those things? How could he be so cruel and callous? How could he look me in the eyes and call me a liar?

Was he right?

Is that why his words felt like a knife in my heart?

Deep down, I know that this is all my fault. It was wrong of me to lie about the tickets in the first place. I thought it would make everything easier—but now it's only made everything worse.

I saw the look in Weston's eyes when he confronted me—

betrayal. He may have sounded angry to anyone else, but I know him inside and out. I know when he's hurt.

But I didn't care. I was so wild and mad, all I wanted to do was unleash my fury on him—give him a taste of his own medicine.

It was more than a taste. It was more like the whole bottle. Poison I didn't even know I possessed. I poured it all out and watched his heart break. And in the moment, it felt so satisfying to yell in his face, to tell him that I hate him.

But I didn't mean it.

Not a word of it.

And now I hate *myself* for saying those things.

Shame consumes my whole being, making me feel tainted and rotten inside. My own words echo through my mind, haunting me.

You're always pushing in where you're not wanted...

always bossing me around like you know best...

You're insufferable.

I was just as cruel as Weston was—worse, because there was no truth to what I said. But there *was* some truth to what he said.

I *have* been purposely evading my mother. I *have* gone out of my way to avoid her, and I used Weston as the excuse. I've done nothing to make things better between me and Mom—instead, I've been carefully keeping my distance.

Afraid of getting too close.

Afraid of being left behind again.

Weston doesn't know what that feels like—to know that your mother doesn't want you. He wonders why I never called her. Why would you call someone who couldn't care less if they hear your voice again?

He doesn't understand.

No one understands.

That's what I tell myself as I lie here alone in the dark, drowning in an ocean of regret, my heart heavy with shame.

But it's not just shame for the way I treated Weston.

It's shame for the way I've treated Mom over these past weeks.

Grandma was right—my mother *has* made some mistakes with her life.

But so have I.

Perhaps nothing as drastic as having a baby... But what if I did?

Mom wasn't much older than I am now when she got pregnant. Did she cry like this when she found out? Did she fight with her boyfriend, like I just have? Did he walk away and leave her feeling even more lost and broken? Did she sob into her pillow and wish she could just crawl into a hole and die? Like I do?

I've tried to put myself in Mom's shoes before. But I could never relate to any part of her story. I always took the moral high ground and argued against her case with righteous indignation.

I always thought: Why did she sleep with her boyfriend in the first place?

But now I know how difficult it is to resist the boy you love when he stands so close to you and his lips are kissing you with dizzying passion.

What if it happened to me?

What if I lost my footing on the moral high ground, slipped and fell... into his bed? What if I surrendered myself to one night of weakness? What if I awoke one morning and found myself pregnant with his baby?

I try to imagine what that would feel like, to have a human being growing inside me. To suddenly be responsible for a child that I didn't ask for, didn't expect.

To be a mother, just like that.

It's a terrifying thought.

I feel like my own life has barely begun.

I still have so much to learn, so much life to live.

Someday, I *do* want to be a mother. In fact, that's part of the "*future* future" I joke about with Weston—the fantasies I amuse myself with sometimes. That we'll get married one day, years from now, and live in a cute house with a cute dog, and I will happily have his babies.

But right now? I'm a mess.

I can't even manage my *own* life.

I can't even get through one Christmas without breaking Weston's heart, destroying every fragment of happiness we had together, and leaving my family to deal with the consequences of my mistakes.

I'm a terrible girlfriend.

A terrible granddaughter.

A terrible *daughter*.

Perhaps I have more in common with Mom than I realized.

Perhaps we both have flaws.

Weaknesses.

Moments that we wish we could go back and live differently.

Weston's voice echoes through my mind, his unanswered question burning on my conscience.

"How many times did you try to fix the problem yourself?"

I avoided answering him.

Because the answer is none.

A good relationship takes two people doing their part.

And I haven't been doing my part.

That's what I now see, as the fog of my anger and bitterness begins to clear, revealing the awful truth.

I've been the selfish one, the irresponsible one.

Too concerned with my own feelings to consider my mother's. Too obsessed with the past to give the future a chance. Too stubborn to see my own shortcomings.

Weston was right—everything he said was right. But it hurt my pride too much to admit it. So instead, I lashed out at him in anger.

Something felt so dreadfully final about our fight. As if we were walking out on each other. Giving up.

Breaking up.

My heart is too heavy to sleep, so I push aside my sheets and get out of bed, tiptoeing downstairs to check on the puppy. I might as well keep Thor company. He's been whining at night—missing his mother, I suppose.

"Shh. It's okay, cutie," I murmur when I find him whimpering on the floor of the laundry room with his nose pressed up against the gate. I pick him up, nuzzling his fuzzy head. "Come on. We can be sad together."

In the living room, I sit on the floor and play quietly with Thor, who forgets about his troubles much more quickly than I can forget about mine. I start a game of tug-of-war with his blanket, and when he gets too excited, I give up—so he doesn't wake my grandparents with all his fierce growling. As he rolls around victoriously with his blanket, something on the coffee table catches my eye.

It's the book Weston gave me, still wrapped in vintage Christmas paper.

It makes my heart sink to remember how happy we were in the bookstore together. How I said it would be so romantic for us to buy a book for each other and open them when we were alone.

Well, I'm alone now.

Too alone.

I take the parcel into my lap and unwrap it. The book is small, a crimson cloth hardcover with gilded edges—a collection of poems by Emily Dickinson, illustrated with pretty botanical artwork on every other page. It brings a smile to my face, just flipping through it.

Weston knows me so well.

On the first page, I find the inscription he left for me. With tears in my eyes and a broken heart in my chest, I read his words.

Tessa,

This is what love means to me:

Wanting to be with you all the time, like you said

Thinking of you the second I wake up in the morning

Dreaming of you at night

Pushing you outside your comfort zone

Watching you fly

and cheering you on

You don't just make my life brighter, Tessa—you light it.

Like the sun.

It's dark without you.

    —W

WESTON

DECEMBER 22

"WESTON?"

Mom's voice, muffled, through my bedroom door. Two soft knocks.

"You awake?"

I am now.

"Mm-hmm," I grumble, dragging a hand over my face.

"You're gonna be late for school if you don't get a move on," Mom says.

School.

I groan, shutting my eyes for just one more minute. My head hurts, and I feel hungover—even though I've never tried alcohol in my life, so I don't actually know what a hangover feels like.

But I'm pretty sure Tessa broke up with me last night.

And bro, that's worse than any hangover you can imagine.

I don't have the energy to go to school.

I don't even have the energy to put my legs on.

All I want to do is go back to sleep—forget about last night, forget about all the things I shouldn't have said, forget about the way Tessa screamed at me with angry tears in her eyes.

Do you know what I hate about you, Weston?

Knock, knock on my door again.

"Sweetheart, your dad's leaving in ten minutes."

"I'm coming," I call back, sitting up to slide my prosthetic socks over my stumps. I get my legs on and dress in all black, then grab my backpack and hurry downstairs. Mom tries to make me eat something, but I tell her I'm not hungry.

I don't say a word the whole ride to school. Dad drives, and I let Henry sit up front because the passenger seat still smells like Tessa's perfume, and I just can't handle that right now.

"You okay, Weston?" Dad asks, meeting my eyes through the rearview mirror.

I shrug. "Headache."

"Mm. Had a little too much fun last night, huh?"

I mutter a lifeless laugh. "Yeah."

If only he was right.

If only I hadn't confronted Tessa.

If only I had left it alone.

If only, if only...

Everything was so good up till that point. Why did I have to go and ruin our night together?

She's right—I don't know when to shut up. I never have.

Maybe I'm just not cut out for this boyfriend thing.

But I can't blindly take Tessa's side in every argument. I can't say that I agree with her when I don't.

Brutal honesty is the only thing I know.

And god, I was brutal, wasn't I?

She stood there in the cold, staring at me while I tore her apart.

Called her a liar. Made her cry.

Guilt twists in my stomach every time I think about it. And all day at school, I can't *stop* thinking about it. I can't focus on any of my classes—not when her voice is stuck in my head, playing on repeat.

You're so arrogant, so rude and offensive. You always have been...

"Wes."

I snap out of it, glancing up at Rudy. We're the only ones in the classroom. Physics must have just ended—I didn't even notice everyone leave.

"You look like hell," Rudy says, sitting on the edge of a desk. "What's going on, man?"

I rub my eyes with the heels of my hands. "Me and Tessa had a fight."

"About what?"

I take a deep breath and spill my guts—starting with the ticket drama and ending with the slamming door. I forget most of what I said to Tessa, but I remember every word she yelled in my face.

Every knife she stuck in my chest.

"She wouldn't have said all that if it wasn't true," I murmur, looking down at my desk. "But you know the worst part? How she said *always*. 'You're *always* doing this; you're *always* doing that...' It wasn't just something I did last night that pissed her off—it's who I am, all the time." I blow out a sigh, shaking my head. "If she really hates all those things about me... then she hates *me.*"

"She doesn't hate you," Rudy says.

"How do you know?"

"Because I've seen you guys together."

"You didn't see her last night," I argue. "I've never seen her so mad before. Not even the first time I met her, when she really *did* hate me."

Rudy shrugs. "Well, you called her out. What did you expect? 'Thank you for your input, Weston—I *have* been treating my mom like dirt.'"

I grunt. "I wasn't expecting *that*. But… I don't know. I thought we could talk about it without her flying off the handle."

"Well, you're not exactly the most subtle guy when it comes to confrontation."

"I just said it like it was."

"See? You can't do that with girls," Rudy says, like an expert dating advisor. "They get offended by the littlest thing."

"So what am I supposed to do? Tiptoe around the frickin' tulips? Is that what you do with Clara?"

"Yep." He nods with emphasis. "And let me tell you, Clara has *many* tulips to tiptoe around."

I laugh dryly. "Well, that's stupid. I'm not gonna do that."

"Well, then you've gotta deal with the consequences, bro."

I groan, tipping my head back and shutting my eyes. "I don't even know what those consequences are. Breaking up? Like, are we done? Are we so weak that one fight rips us apart?"

Rudy doesn't reply. I've gone out of his depth now—asking questions that only a fortune-teller could answer.

"Maybe it's for the best," I say quietly. "If that's how she really feels about me, I'd rather know now than go another day believing in something that isn't real."

"Hey. Don't be so dramatic. We all say stuff we don't mean when we're angry."

"Yeah, I guess so."

Rudy straightens up, clapping a hand on my shoulder. "If I were you, I'd give her some time. That's usually all it takes. I bet you twenty bucks she'll call you tonight, crying about how sorry she is."

I'm not so sure about that. But I manage to give him a humorless smile and say, "Well, I could use twenty bucks after last night."

❄ ❄ ❄

She doesn't call me.

She doesn't even text.

I'm refreshing our thread all day, hoping it's something wrong with my phone and that's why I haven't heard from her.

But I know that's not why.

I know she's still angry with me. And I wonder if we'll ever make up.

Sure, it's been less than twenty-four hours since we fought. But Tessa never admits when she's wrong. And I can't apologize for something I didn't do. Maybe I used the wrong tone of voice with her, but I meant every word I said.

I can't take any of it back. It was the truth. And if we can't be truthful with each other, what kind of relationship do we really have?

When Dad picks me up from school, he hands me the book Tessa gave me last night. I must have left it in the truck—I forgot all about it in the aftermath of our fight.

Now I take the book up to my room and unwrap it. *Make Your Bed*, by Admiral William H. McRaven. It looks like some kind of motivational nonfiction book, and it's super short, so that's a plus. I almost laugh at the title. Was Tessa trying to make some kind of dig at my messy room?

Ironically, my bed is *not* made right now.

When I open the book, I find a note from Tessa written on the first page. Funny, I did the same thing in *her* book. I guess great minds really do think alike.

To my sweet Weston,

I hope this book inspires you half as much as you inspire me.

Love forever and always,

Tessa

xoxo

It only makes everything hurt more, to see my name in her handwriting. To hear those words in her voice.

Forever and always.

How can people say that? We don't know what "forever" looks like. We don't even know what tomorrow looks like.

I make my bed, because it seems wrong *not* to, with that book now sitting on my nightstand. There's a ton of homework piling up on my desk, but I don't have the strength to do anything except lie on my bed and scroll through photos on my phone. Photos of me and Tessa.

A lot of them are pictures she took and sent to me—hundreds of snapshots from the past months. All those happy memories, each one like a twist of a knife. I probably shouldn't be doing this to myself, but I can't help it.

I remember what Tessa said when we were looking at those old photo albums together, weeks ago. She said it's like reliving a moment in time that will never happen again.

Never.

I hate that word. It's the sharpest knife of all, and I can't get it out of my head. I have to pick up that book again and open it to the first page and look at her note.

Forever and always.

That's how long I'll love her. Even if she doesn't feel the same way about me anymore. Even if she breaks up with me.

Never.

That's how long it will take for me to get over her.

I already miss her like hell, and I haven't even gone a day without her.

How do people survive this?

I have more respect for all those sappy breakup songs—I get it now. The thought of losing Tessa freaks me out more than anything has since the amputation.

Actually, it feels a lot like that day I found out I was going to lose my legs. The same questions race through my mind.

How will I be able to live like that?

How will I do any of the things I used to do?

How will I ever be happy again?

Looking at the photos of me and Tessa, I know that I won't. Nothing will be the same without her. What I wrote in her book was true—she's my sunlight. How can I live without her?

I can't.

My vision blurs, and I press my eyes shut—feeling like a pansy-ass when the tears start sliding down my face.

TESSA

DECEMBER 22

WHEN I COME DOWNSTAIRS ON THURSDAY MORNING, I realize that Mom must have told Grandma and Grandpa about the fight. No one asks me where I got the dark circles under my eyes—and they don't breathe a word about Weston. They are uncharacteristically quiet and subdued, as if they've all collectively agreed to give me space today and let me be sad.

We still don't have a Christmas tree, so in the afternoon I go with Grandpa to the Mercantile and help him pick one out. There are only four trees left to choose from, so we take the least shabby one: a lopsided Fraser fir with fragrant, silvery-green boughs.

We bring the tree home and decorate it with all the trimmings Grandma has kept since Mom was a little girl—long strings of shiny gold beads, ribbon chain garland, vintage bulbs, and hand-painted ornaments from my childhood. Mom gets a thrill out of seeing all the stuff I made when I was little, and says she wishes she had been there for all those Christmases.

I wish she had, too.

But there's no point in regretting what's past, is there?

Unfortunately, regret comes as naturally to me as breathing. I help decorate the tree, but my heart's not in it. Not like the day I went with the Ludovicos to get *their* tree. Later on, Grandma and Mom bake sugar cookies, just for us this time, but I don't have the energy to help.

It reminds me too much of Weston. How he made me laugh that day, when I was in such a sour mood. How he picked me up and put me on the counter and kissed me.

All afternoon, I'm staring at my phone, thinking about calling him—but I never actually do. I'm too ashamed of myself. Too lost at sea to do anything except lie on the couch and snuggle Thor and wish I were snuggling Weston instead.

It makes me want to cry when I think about how happy we were.

How I wanted to make this the best Christmas ever.

Now it is undoubtedly the *worst* Christmas ever.

And it's all my fault.

These are the anxieties that haunt me as I get into bed that night. I lie awake in the dark, again, hopelessly waiting for the butterflies of sleep to come and carry me away from my misery.

I'm wearing Weston's hoodie, which is the closest I can get to being hugged by him right now. But even his smell is starting to fade from the fabric, and that makes my heart hurt even more.

Giving up on sleep, I climb out of bed and go downstairs to check on Thor. Sure enough, he's whining again—nose pressed against the gate, crying for his mommy.

"Oh, baby," I coax softly, lifting him up in my arms. "You gotta stop being so sad…"

I bring him into the living room and cuddle him by the fireplace. Grandpa had it blazing festively earlier this evening, but now all that remains of the fire is a pile of glowing embers. I rub Thor's belly and whisper, "It's okay… you won't always miss your mama."

That's when I hear soft footsteps on the stairs. Mom steps into the living room, wearing pajamas and a surprised expression.

"Tessa? You're still up?"

"No, I… couldn't sleep. And neither could Thor."

Mom gives the puppy a sympathetic pout, then comes to sit on the couch beside me.

"Poor little thing." She sighs, scratching Thor's fuzzy ears. "I remember holding *you* like this when you were first born." She smiles a little at the recollection. "You *hated* being alone in your crib. You'd cry and cry until I picked you up. The only way I could get you to fall asleep was to rock you and sing to you. I remember watching your beautiful little face as you drifted off…"

I swallow, a lump in my throat as tears begin stinging my eyes.

"The one song that always made you fall asleep was 'Rock-a-bye baby.'" She reaches up to tuck a strand of hair behind my ear. And then, softly, she starts to sing it to me again. "*Rock-a-bye baby, on the tree top…*"

I break down crying.

The hurting just wells up inside me until it is more than I can bear. It spills out of me in a sob, and the next thing I know I am wrapping my arms around my mother and crying into her neck.

Everything is a blur. I'm choking on my tears, and Mom is rubbing my back, and suddenly my anger is melting away, like ice in the heat of the sun.

"I'm so sorry, Mom," I sob into her hair. "I've been so awful to you, and I'm sorry…"

"It's okay, honey," she says, her own voice wobbling with tears. "I understand. And *I'm* the one who should be sorry." She pulls back to look at me—to cup my tear-streaked face in her hands. "I never wanted to leave you, my baby."

"Then why did you?" I choke out in a whisper.

"Because I thought it was for the best. I wanted you to have a good childhood—a good *life*. I wanted you to have a family and a home... And I couldn't give you that. But I knew the best parents in the world, and they were in need of a daughter. A *good* daughter." Mom smiles a little, tears glimmering in her eyes. "To make up for the one they lost."

I sniff, swiping tears off my face. "I thought it was me. I thought you didn't want me. I thought..." My throat tightens, but I force the words out anyway—no matter how much they hurt. "I thought I wasn't good enough for you, somehow..."

"Oh, honey, no. Absolutely not." She wraps me in a tight hug, kissing my hair. "The best thing I ever did in my life... was bring you into this world."

My heart breaks like a crumbling dam, and out of me rushes all the pain I didn't know I had been holding onto for so long. I collapse against my mother and cry, silent and breathless—holding onto her while she holds onto me.

"I just wanted you to be happy," Mom whispers. "That's why I left. Because I knew you would all be better off without me."

"How could you think that? I needed you... I *need* you." My voice loses its strength, and all I can do is whisper into her hair. "I'm so sorry for the way I've treated you these past weeks. I'm ashamed of myself."

Mom chuckles a little, as though this is no great calamity. "It's alright, Tessa."

"No, it's not. Can you forgive me?"

"If *you* can forgive *me*," Mom says.

I nod, holding her close. "I can. I do. With all my heart."

For a few minutes, we sit there hugging each other—wordless, weeping. I feel like such a weight has been lifted off me, and that's when I realize how exhausting and burdensome it is to hold onto a grudge.

"You know," Mom says at last, "that sweet boyfriend of yours told me that I should move here."

I pull back to stare at her. "Weston said that?"

Mom nods. "I didn't think it was such a good idea at the time. But now—"

"He's right," I interrupt. "You should. I don't want you to go back to Pittsburgh. I want you to stay."

A little smile finds Mom's face. "That's what Weston said."

"He knows me so well... better than I know myself." I dissolve into tears again, burying my face in my hands. "Oh, Mom, I said such terrible things to him last night... and I didn't mean any of it, but I hurt him—I could tell I did, and now he probably hates me."

"I don't think so." Mom laughs gently, stroking my hair. "In fact, I know for certain that he loves you very, very much."

"That makes it even worse," I whimper into my hands. "Because I'm a brute, and I don't deserve him..."

Thor nudges me with his cold little nose, as if trying to cheer me up.

"That's not true," Mom reassures me. "We all make mistakes, honey. It's part of being in love."

"I thought love was supposed to be wonderful."

"Not always. Sometimes it's messy and shitty and you wish you'd never fallen for the boy in the first place."

I shake my head. "I never wish that. I wouldn't trade Weston for the whole world."

"Why don't you tell him that?" Mom says, rubbing my shoulder. "You'll feel better if you apologize for yelling at him."

"Was I yelling?"

Mom nods, stifling a smirk. "Well, I could hear you from inside the house."

A sad laugh tumbles out of me. "Poor Wes…"

He was only trying to help me, and I treated him with contempt.

They say hindsight is twenty-twenty—and now, I can see that I wasn't even angry with *Weston*—I was angry with myself. But I took it out on him.

"I need to tell him how sorry I am," I say, brushing the tears off my cheeks. "But I can't do it over the phone. I need to see him in person."

Mom falls silent for a moment; then she comes up with a suggestion. "How about we go shopping tomorrow morning—just me and you. And afterwards, I can drop you off at Weston's house, and you can make up… and make out."

A surprised laugh bursts past my lips. "I'd like that. The shopping, I mean. Actually, I've been wanting to buy something special to wear on Christmas Eve. If his parents still want to have us over, that is."

"I'm sure they will." Mom gives me a reassuring smile. "Everything will look brighter in the morning."

Mom was right.

Everything *does* look brighter in the morning.

For one thing, the sun is shining—rays of gold pour through my bedroom window as I open my eyes. I take it as a good omen, and it brings a smile to my face. I feel as light as a feather as I spring out of bed and get ready for my shopping escapade with Mom.

It's a new day.

Really, truly *new*.

And it feels like the first new day I've lived in a very long time.

Grandma and Grandpa are all smiles when I show my face downstairs. But Mom gets the first good morning kiss—and my grandparents don't mind at all. In fact, I've never seen them happier.

After breakfast, Mom and I take off for the mall. Mom drives, and I put on the playlist Weston made for me, and we both respectively swoon over how adorable he is.

When we arrive at the mall, we decide to start with the most fun part: dress shopping. Mom and I load up our arms with dresses of all different colors and lengths; then we spend ages in the fitting room as I try them on.

Most of the dresses are too *something*:

"Too formal," Mom says as I model a light blue tulle gown that goes all the way to the floor.

"I agree."

Next: a sparkly blush pink one that's not quite as long.

"Too sequined?" I wonder, blinding myself as I look at all that glitter in the mirror.

Mom laughs. "Yeah…"

Next: a satiny dark green dress that hits me at the knees and has just the right amount of sparkle.

"Too expensive!" I gasp, noticing the tag that reads $289. "It's not *that* pretty."

The next one is so immodest I don't dare to even step outside the dressing room. It's an elegant red mermaid dress, which fits me surprisingly well—but hugs every curve of my body. And to make matters worse, it's strapless.

"Did you pick this one out?" I ask Mom through the door.

"Which one? Show me."

"No. It's too sexy."

Mom chuckles. "Oh, I'm sure it's not."

I open the door to show her. "Look at this neckline."

She gives me a once-over and grins. "Well... I think *Weston* would like it."

"Mom!" I blush as red as the fabric, swinging the door shut and hastily stripping the dress off.

The next one is more my style—crimson red, tea-length, with a far more modest sweetheart neckline. The whole dress has a vintage, Hepburn flair and just enough sequins—sparkling around the bodice and thinning out as the skirt flows down around my knees.

I know it's the one before I open the door and show Mom. Her eyes widen, and she says, "That's *so* you."

I giggle, twirling around. "Is it modest enough?"

Mom grunts. "*Too* modest, if you ask me. But it's very flattering. You're beautiful, Tessa."

I bite my lip, examining myself in the mirror. "Do you think Weston will like it?"

"Like it? Honey, he's gonna drop dead."

I laugh and roll my eyes, but I secretly cannot wait for Weston to see me in it.

Mom insists on buying the dress for me. "An early Christmas gift," she says, to make me feel better. Thankfully, it's under a hundred dollars. But still, I'm super grateful and shower her in thank-yous as we exit the store.

"If you're going to pay for the dress, then *I'm* buying us lunch," I say, and Mom doesn't fight me on this. So I take her to my favorite cafe, and that's where we sort out all the Christmas gifts we need to buy.

It's not until we're wandering back through the mall that I confess, "I still don't have a gift for Weston."

"Really?" Mom raises an eyebrow. "I thought you'd have had that all planned out long ago."

"I know," I groan, shaking my head. "But I wanted to get him something really *special*, you know? I just... never figured out what that thing is, and now I'm almost out of time!"

Mom thinks for a moment, scanning the storefronts as we walk. "Well, I think you've already got the perfect gift for him, hidden right under your nose."

"Really? What?"

Mom grins. "Those secret poems."

My heart jumps. "The ones about Weston?"

Mom nods. "Can't get much more romantic than that."

"But they're so... personal."

"All the more reason," Mom says. "I think it would do him good to see how you really feel... How much you care about him."

I look down. "Because of the fight?"

"Yeah, and..." Mom trails off and never finishes that thought. Instead, she says, "Well, it never hurts to have a reminder, does it?"

"No. No, I suppose it doesn't." I follow her into a store, absent-mindedly fingering clothes as I walk past them. "You're right. I *should* give him the poems. It's unique, anyway. Something only I could give."

"Exactly."

Hopefully the poems *will* have that effect and show him how I really feel about him. But first, I need to apologize. I need to mend the breach between us.

I need to kiss him. And I'm not sure I can wait until he gets out of school.

WESTON

DECEMBER 23

I FINALLY HAVE AN IDEA FOR TESSA'S CHRISTMAS GIFT: a photo album, for our memories together. No, it's not amazing or even impressive. But Tessa would probably love it. And it's technically something only I could give her, so that checks the "special" box well enough, I guess.

But now it's too late.

Tessa still hasn't called me or texted me. All last night I was thinking about sending *her* a message—but then I thought about the possibility that she wouldn't respond. And that struck me as being even worse than not communicating at all.

Are we done? I don't know. And I *hate* not knowing. I hate feeling like I have no control over this situation. No power to make things better, no place I can run to, to get away from the looming shadow of my greatest fear.

Tessa is the one who slammed the door, the one who shut me out. I don't know if it's just my pride, but I can't bring myself to go banging on that door, begging for her to open up and talk to me.

Yeah, I miss her like hell.

But I want her to miss *me* like hell.

If she doesn't, I'd rather swallow that bitter pill now and try to move on with my life...

But is that even possible without her?

✳ ✳ ✳

It's the day before winter break, so everything at school is pretty chill and casual. Nobody cares much about anything they're doing; we just go through the motions, waiting for it to be over.

I sit next to Shiori again in lab, and today she has her black hair in two long braids, tied with little pink bows.

"Are you okay, Weston?" she says, when I don't talk for a record-breaking five minutes.

"Yeah." I nod. "Never been better. Why?"

"It's just... you look sad. You're usually all smiles."

I'm not about to spill my relationship problems to her, so instead I force a smile to make up for my apparent lack of Christmas cheer and say, "I'm fine. Thanks for asking."

I turn back to my chemistry notebook, flipping aimlessly through the pages. I can't even remember what we're supposed to be doing.

"Soooo," Shiori says, pinning her manicured fingertip down on my notebook so I can't turn the next page.

I glance up at her, raising an eyebrow.

"Are you going to winter formal?" she asks, and I can tell there's a special reason she's asking.

"Probably not," I say. "My girlfriend's not really into stuff like that."

Shiori's face falls. "Oh. You... have a girlfriend?"

I give her a weak smile, seeing that I just stepped on one of her tulips. "Yeah. That is... I think I do. She's not really speaking to me at the moment."

"Oh. I'm sorry to hear that."

But she actually looks kind of thrilled to hear that.

I don't find out why until the end of seventh period when I'm emptying out my locker and Rudy punches my shoulder.

"Hey."

I straighten up, shoving some folders into my backpack. "Before you ask, no—she didn't call me. Didn't text either. And I have no idea what it means."

"Actually," Rudy says, "I wasn't going to ask you about Tessa. I knew you'd tell me the second she called, so..."

I shoot him a glare, swinging my locker shut. "What is it, then?"

"Remember that survey you did last week? Asking a bunch of girls about their crushes?"

A tired laugh stumbles out of me. "Yeah. Load of good it did. I can't figure girls out no matter how hard I try."

Rudy doesn't reply to that one. He just looks at me like he's in on some joke I don't know about.

I frown suspiciously. "What's that smirk for?"

He crosses his arms smugly and leans back against the lockers. "I decided to conduct a little social experiment of my own. Well, Clara helped a lot—she asked the question."

I'm all ears now. "What question?"

"Who do you wish would ask you to winter formal?"

"Me?" I say, confused.

Rudy sighs. "No, not *you*. I'm saying Clara asked all her friends that question—all the girls you talked to last week. And guess how many of them said 'Weston'?"

I grunt. "None."

That's when Rudy pulls a piece of paper out of his pocket and hands it to me. "You greatly underestimate your popularity, bro."

I frown, unfolding the paper and finding a list of girls' names—a pretty long list.

"Bullshit. You're making this up."

Rudy shakes his head. "I'm not, swear to God. Check your survey. You'll find that my list perfectly coincides with the girls who refused to tell you their crush's name. Weird, huh?"

No way.

I look more closely at the list, immediately recognizing some of the girls I talked to last week. Violet Robinson, McKenzie Newman, Shiori Ono, Candace Hayes—

"Hayes?" I almost choke. "No way she said she likes me."

Rudy laughs. "Clara had to drag it out of her, but yeah. True story."

I remember how snarky and defensive Candace was when I asked her about her crush. Was that because the guy she was describing was... *me*? I barely remember what she said, something about him having a good sense of humor. And now that I think about it, I *am* one of the only people who can make her laugh.

Shiori is no surprise—I could tell she had a crush on me by how bummed she was to hear that I already have a girlfriend. Apparently not many girls know this small detail about me.

I start to realize that Rudy is right. Smart-ass.

"Why did you and Clara go to all this trouble?" I ask, glancing up from the paper.

"To prove a point."

"What point?"

"That you already are the guy you're trying to be," Rudy says, slapping me on the shoulder. "So stop trying."

I laugh, shaking my head.

How is this possible?

How can I be so popular without even knowing it?

I guess I always figured that girls stare at me for only one reason.

I guess I was wrong.

"Also," Rudy adds, "if Tessa ends up being... not worthy of you—" he gives me a sharp look "—just remember, you have a waiting list."

I smile weakly. "I don't think so, Kaufmann." I shove the note into my backpack and head down the crowded hall. Rudy follows me. "I mean, don't get me wrong—it's nice to know all these girls have a crush on me. Like, what guy wouldn't want that? But to be honest, it means nothing if I don't have Tessa. She's the only girl I could ever love. Nobody would be able to replace her."

"Well, why don't you tell her that?"

I sigh, turning around to face Rudy. "If she called me or texted me, I *would* tell her that. But she hasn't."

Rudy's gaze catches on something over my shoulder. "And... do *you* want to talk to *her*?"

"Of course. But she doesn't want to talk to *me*. She probably doesn't want to see me ever again."

"Well, I doubt she's here to see *me*."

I freeze. "What?"

Rudy just grins and says, "Turn around."

I do.

And there's Tessa standing by the entrance doors, sunlight pouring through the glass and making her hair glow. She's glancing around at everything like an astronaut who just landed on a foreign planet—

and I have to admit, that's how out of place she looks at school. Her eyes lock on mine across the hallway, and her name crosses my lips in a whisper.

Rudy makes himself scarce as Tessa approaches me, an unsure little smile curving onto her face. My heart starts beating faster, and I hope to God this isn't the breakup.

"Tessa? What are you doing here?"

She stops, a few feet of space between us. "I had to see you. To tell you…" Her voice wavers, and she shakes her head, looking close to tears. "I'm so, *so* sorry. You were right about everything. And I was… I was so wrong. I said some terrible things to you, and I can't remember most of them, but I want you to know that I didn't mean any of it. I was just so mad because I knew you were right and I was wrong."

A relieved sigh comes rushing out of me, and I shut my eyes for a second—feeling like the weight of the whole damn world has just been lifted off my chest.

"Well, you weren't totally wrong," I say. "I *am* arrogant. And I don't think before I open my mouth. And I don't care who I offend, which probably makes me a rude ass—"

"No," Tessa cuts in, grabbing my hand. She looks straight into my eyes and says, "You're confident. And fierce. And honest. And those are all the things I *love* about you, Weston."

Great. Now *I'm* getting choked up.

Tessa is, too. Her eyes are glossy as she leans closer and says in a soft voice, "You're the only one who saves me from myself. You always have been."

I look down at our hands, together again. "You saved me, too."

Tessa smiles, tears cresting in her eyes. "Isn't that what love is all about? Saving each other? Even if it hurts sometimes…" She glances down, rubbing her thumb over my knuckles. "I never thought it *would* hurt. I thought love would be… perfect. But it's not. It doesn't always come easy; sometimes it's hard work. Sometimes it means overcoming challenges. But I think we're both pretty good at that, by this point."

I breathe a tired laugh. "Yeah, I'd say so."

"I overcame it with Mom," Tessa says, her eyes glowing. "I forgave her. And she forgave me, for being so cold and bitter these past few weeks. We've decided to start over."

I smile. "I'm glad to hear that."

"Can we start over, too?"

"Of course we can," I say, wrapping her in a hug. Her arms circle around me, and she holds me tight for a long moment.

"I'm sorry, Tessa… I know I came at you like a bulldozer."

She laughs a little, into my chest. "I'm used to it."

"But I never wanted to hurt you."

"I never wanted to hurt *you*." She sniffs, easing back a little to look me in the eyes. "But I know I did. And I'm ashamed of myself."

I guess I'm not as good at hiding my feelings as I thought. Or maybe it's just Tessa who can see right through me. See my heart. Like I can see hers.

"Don't be ashamed of yourself, Tes. It's okay—really."

She shakes her head. "It's not okay. It was wrong. And I'm sorry." She smiles a little, sliding her hands around my neck. "Will this make up for it?"

She kisses me. Right there in the hallway, in front of everyone.

At first, it startles me—like those dreams where you show up at school naked. But Tessa doesn't care, apparently. She just pops up on her tiptoes and plants her lips on mine, like she wants everyone to know that I'm taken.

Oh, hell yes.

Her sweet smell fills my lungs as her arms loop around my neck, and it feels so good I forget about everything else. I kiss her back unapologetically—holding her by the waist as the rest of the world falls away.

I'm still hers.

She's still mine.

And I'm never letting her go.

❄ ❄ ❄

Operation Christmas Eve Dinner Party is a go—which means Mom is running around like a chicken with its head cut off, trying to make sure everything is perfect. It's all "You boys get your crap off this table" and "Can't somebody clean this house other than me?" and I don't know why she thinks it's such a mess—everything looks fine to me.

I spend most of the day getting Tessa's gift ready—and giving new meaning to the phrase "last minute." Luckily, the Walgreens employees don't get a break on Christmas Eve, so I'm able to get all the pictures I need printed and slap together the photo album in a few hours. It's only about a quarter filled up when I'm done, but I leave the rest of the pages blank for a reason.

When I get back home, I find Mom freaking out over dinner and Dad trying to help her and the boys milling around, getting in her way. She gives me a long list of stuff to do as soon as I walk through the door, so I don't have a chance to wrap Tessa's gift. I can't remember what time Tessa and her family are going to show up, but I'm afraid the question alone would send Mom into a panic attack. Instead, I follow her orders without complaint.

"Finished lighting the candles," I say, finding Mom in the kitchen. "What else can I do?"

Mom doesn't hear me because she's got her head in the oven, poking at some dish. Henry sees me in my hoodie and joggers and blurts, "Hey, how come Weston gets to wear normal clothes and I don't?"

I suddenly notice that he's dressed like he's going to someone's wedding. Actually, everyone is dressed like that.

Henry rolls his eyes and goes, "I'm changing. This is dumb—"

Mom pulls her head out of the oven and grabs his arm. "Don't you dare. Weston, what do you think you're wearing? Go get changed! I told you, semiformal!"

I groan. "What? You're kidding..."

She's not kidding. She makes a sharp shooing motion with one hand, and I grudgingly head for the stairs.

"Hurry up!" Mom yells after me. "They're going to be here soon!"

I hate this dressing-up crap, but I make an effort for Mom's sake. And, obviously, I want to look good for Tessa. She dresses fancy even when there's no requirement to, which means she'll look like a million bucks tonight—and I want to at least *attempt* to look like I deserve her. (Because, really? I don't deserve her.)

I rifle through my dresser drawers and closet for something "semiformal," but all I succeed in doing is making a mess. Muttering cusses under my breath, I rip off my shirt and decide to go with a white button-down under a black vest—it will have to be classy enough for Mom's dress code, because I'm not going anywhere near a tie.

In the bathroom, I mess my hair up with some gel the way Tessa likes it. Luckily, I don't smell bad—because there's no time for a shower. Instead, I steal a drop of Dad's aftershave to go with the quasi–James Bond outfit.

"How's this?" I ask Mom once I'm back in the kitchen.

She approves, a big smile melting her panic for a minute. "That's perfect. You look very handsome, Weston."

"You smell like Dad," Aidan points out, which of course makes Noah come over and chime in, "Yeah, you smell like Dad," which of course makes Mom laugh because she knows why I smell like Dad. I feel my face heat up, but I just grab Noah and throw him over my shoulder. He flails in a giggling rage as I carry him off to the living room, where Dad is tossing more wood into the blazing fireplace.

There's always this weird limbo before people show up for a party—nobody really knows what to do with themselves, because you don't know how much time you actually have before your doorbell rings. I let Noah wrestle me on the couch for a few minutes because that's always a good way to kill time—then finally he gets me in a headlock and forces me to tell him what I got Tessa for Christmas.

"A photo album," I confess through a mouthful of pillows. "But don't you dare tell her."

Noah lets me out of the chokehold, and when I straighten up, he's blinking at me, disappointed. "That's boring. I thought you were gonna ask her to marry you."

I laugh and ruffle his hair. "Not this year, buddy."

That's when I hear a car pull into our driveway. Headlights on the curtains.

"They're here!" I holler to Mom, springing off the couch and straightening the pillows that she probably had perfect before Noah and I got to them. I try to straighten my shirt and vest as Dad goes to answer the door.

A gust of cold air pours in the house along with a chaos of voices, everyone talking over each other. Aidan and Noah run over to shout,

"Merry Christmas!" at everyone, but I hang back in the hallway, my heartbeat hammering in my chest as I wait to see Tessa.

There—her blue eyes are sparkling, and I can tell that she's smiling, but she's hidden behind her mom, and I can't really see her until everyone starts filing inside and Tessa is standing alone.

That's when my heart forgets how to beat.

TESSA

DECEMBER 24

I SPEND CHRISTMAS EVE AFTERNOON COPYING DOWN all my love poems into a new unlined Moleskine notebook. I'm going to give it to Weston tonight instead of waiting for tomorrow morning. There will be too many people around on Christmas Day, and I don't want everyone watching while I give this special piece of my heart to him. I certainly don't want anyone *reading* the poems except him. Besides, Christmas Eve is a far more romantic time to exchange gifts.

When I've finished, I give the book a tiny spritz of perfume, like posh ladies used to do with their love letters—then I wrap the little book in Christmas paper and slip it into my bag for tonight.

I start getting ready long before I need to. Mom and I watch *It's a Wonderful Life* and eat sugar cookies while I paint my fingernails crimson to match my dress.

When we have three hours still to go, I start on my hairstyle. With Mom's help and tons of photos from Pinterest, I succeed in arranging my hair into an elegant braided bun, complete with a few tiny sprigs of baby's breath tucked into the folds of my blonde curls. Mom pulls out two wispy strands to parenthesize my face.

"You're so good with hair," I tell her as I admire the final result in my hand mirror.

Mom chuckles and says, "I used to be."

I complete the outfit with pearl earrings and black ballet flats, glossing my lips with a ruby-tinted lip balm. I really hope I haven't overdone it. Mrs. Ludovico *did* say this was to be a special dinner party, which usually calls for semiformal dress.

"You look so beautiful!" Grandma gasps when I come down the stairs, smiling and blushing.

"Doesn't she?" Mom says, making me twirl around to show off my dress. It's the first time my grandparents have seen me in it, and I'm happy they both approve.

"I feel like we should be taking you to a ball," Grandpa says with a chuckle. He's wearing his church clothes and looks every bit as formal as I do, which makes me feel better about the glittery dress.

I grin, turning to give Mom a kiss on the cheek. "Thank you again for the dress... For everything."

She squeezes my hand and says, "I love you."

"I love you, too."

❄ ❄ ❄

It's snowing when we arrive at the Ludovicos' house—a graceful, perfect Hollywood snow that seems to be falling just for the aesthetic. Their house looks so adorable and cozy, even from the outside—twinkle lights cresting the eaves of the porch and candles glowing in the windows. The whole scene looks like a Currier and Ives Christmas card.

I follow my mom and grandparents up the porch steps and inside. Mr. Ludovico welcomes us, his voice drowned out by a cacophony of "Merry Christmases" from Weston's little brothers, who look so cute all dressed up. My heartbeat quickens as I glance around, searching for Weston.

That's when our eyes meet. And suddenly no one else exists.

He is, without a doubt, the handsomest boy I have ever seen. He's wearing a white button-down shirt with a black vest; his sleeves are cuffed halfway up to reveal his suntanned forearms; his hair is so perfectly messy it practically begs me to come bury my hands in it. His black trousers and vest give him the look of a vintage prep school boy, and I'm officially obsessed with this style on Weston.

For a long moment, we just stare at each other, too far apart to speak. Our families disperse into the living room, but Weston and I stay behind in the foyer, frozen in place. At last, I awaken from my moonstruck daze and approach him.

"Tessa," he says softly, his gaze tracing my body, "you look... stunning."

I stifle a smile, giddy feelings lighting up inside me. "So do you," I whisper, still taking him in. "I'm kind of in shock right now... I've never seen you dressed so nice."

He grins. "I'm in shock, too." I start to blush at the compliment, but then he adds, "I've never seen myself look so hot."

I scoff, turning away and crossing my arms in feigned offense.

Weston laughs that contagious laugh of his, pulling me in by the waist and leaning close to my ear. "Just kidding. I'm in shock because you are the most beautiful girl in the world, and I have no idea what I ever did to deserve you."

I stifle a smile, trying to give him a stern look. "I have no idea, either."

He glances at my lips, and it stirs up a storm of butterflies in my stomach. It's no use. He's too close and too adorable, and he smells too good—even better than usual, if that's possible. There's something muskier and more grown-up about his scent tonight, and I can't resist him a second longer—

"Tessa!" Mrs. Ludovico bursts in with a smile.

Weston and I fly apart—blushing fiercely.

His mother would have caught us kissing if she had waited a moment longer. I nervously clear my throat and exchange hellos with her, complimenting her on how lovely she looks as she compliments me on how lovely *I* look.

"Come on in, you two," she says, passing Weston a meaningful little smile that makes him nervously fumble with his hair.

I turn to follow his mother into the living room, but Weston grabs my wrist and pulls me back into his arms.

"That was anticlimactic."

I giggle. "Shh. We can't just stay out here kissing and avoiding everyone."

"Why not? Sounds like a good time."

"We can do that later. Actually, I was hoping I could give you my gift tonight. When we're alone."

Weston raises one eyebrow. "Alone?"

"Yeah, well, I don't want your parents and all your brothers watching while you open it."

"Why? What is it?"

I sigh. "I'm not gonna *tell you*. It's just something that's... for your eyes only."

Weston smirks in that devilish way of his. "My imagination is running wild."

I roll my eyes.

He falls silent, thinking about it for a moment before saying, "I think I'll give you mine, too. It's also for your eyes only."

My heart flutters, glowing in my chest like all the twinkle lights put together. "Really?"

"Well, I mean, it's not much, but—"

"I'm sure I'll love it. Okay, so let's sneak away at some point when everyone's distracted with something else."

Weston nods. "Sounds good."

"Where should we meet? Your room?"

He gives me a little smirk. "That... might raise some eyebrows."

It takes a second before I understand his meaning. "Oh! Right. Yeah..." I shake my head, my cheeks going all warm. "That wouldn't be good."

"Not that we would be doing anything wrong—"

"No, of course not."

"Just making out."

"Exactly—" I realize what he just said and startle. "Weston!" I smack his arm, but we're both grinning. "Come on, be serious for two seconds. Where should we meet? The den?"

He nods. "Sure."

"We should have a secret signal so we can slip away without being noticed. How about this..." I touch my ear, sliding my fingertips down to fiddle with my pearl earring. "If you see me do that, it means we should slip away."

Weston frowns. "So you're the one who gets to decide when?"

"Alright, fine—you can do it too if you think it's the right moment. But I don't want anyone to see us leave together."

He winks. "Don't worry. Stealth is my middle name."

I grunt, taking his hand in mine. "I thought 'Bulldozer' was your middle name."

He laughs.

The whole house swells with delicious smells, familiar laughter, and all the festive warmth of a Christmas celebration with the people you love most in all the world. A picturesque fire snaps and sizzles in the hearth; the tree we decorated sparkles beside it; soft Christmas piano music plays in the background. Weston's mom pays attention to detail, and I admire that.

I sneak into the kitchen and ask her if I can help with anything, but she shoos me back into the living room to mingle and "enjoy myself." There are fancy hors d'oeuvres and kid-friendly champagne (sparkling cider); we drink the latter out of pretty crystal glasses. Weston looks especially like a posh boy from Oxford University now, as he leans against the wall pretentiously swirling his fake champagne in his wineglass.

I'm across the room, talking to his father, and when I finally look back to Weston, I find him already looking at me—a little amused smirk on his face. He reaches up and touches his ear.

I give him a sharp look, like, *Not yet!*

He sighs, disappointed, and downs the rest of his drink like it's a shot of alcohol. I laugh, nearly choking on mine.

For a while, I enjoy playing hard to get—milling about the kitchen, talking and laughing and letting Weston follow me around, trying to get my attention back. I'm not sure why, but it's extremely satisfying to tease him. He'll have *all* my attention later, so I rather enjoy depriving him of it now.

There's something so wonderfully heartwarming about watching our two families getting to know each other better—everything a jubilant chaos of voices and laughter and little boys chasing each other around the dining table. I can't help but feel like we're all one big family already. I hope it stays this way forever.

Of course, no Christmas gathering with my boyfriend's family would be complete without someone forcing us to kiss under the mistletoe. There's a small bunch of it hanging in the doorway that I happen to be standing under, and Mrs. Ludovico is the first to notice this irony.

"Oh, Tessa," she says with a smirk, "look what's over your head!"

That's when I glance up and see the mistletoe. A little surprised laugh bursts out of me, and I look to Weston, raising my eyebrows expectantly. He sees where this is going and groans, dragging a hand over his reddening face.

Now everyone is chuckling and watching us.

My mom calls out, "Come on, Weston! What are you waiting for?"

I giggle, crooking my finger to beckon him over. He shuffles hesitantly towards me—looking like he wants to melt through the floor. I'm not used to seeing this side of him. Weston is always so confident and bold when he's kissing me anywhere else; but now, in front of his parents, he's all nervous and bashful. For some reason, this makes me want to kiss him even more.

"You're blushing," I whisper, trying not to smile.

"I'm aware of the fact, thank you."

We kiss, quickly and chastely—but romantically enough to satisfy the adults. They all applaud and croon, "Awww," and Weston's brothers make gagging noises. I laugh, looping my arms around his neck.

"Merry Christmas, Weston."

He smiles. "Merry Christmas, Tessa."

For the rest of the evening, Weston tries to convince me to sneak away with him—at all the wrong moments.

His second attempt comes right after dinner—literally as *soon* as I finish eating. He's sitting next to me, so he grabs my hand to get my attention, and when I look up, he's indiscreetly fingering his ear and giving me pleading eyes.

I kick him under the table.

But he only grins and leans closer to my ear. "I can't feel that, you know."

I roll my eyes. "Not yet," I hiss. "It would be rude to leave right now. And *everyone* would notice."

Next, we have dessert and coffee, which I help arrange if only to evade Weston's incorrigible looks and questions. He's beginning to tempt me with that adorable puppy face of his, so I play a little game of musical chairs and swap seats with Mom.

He pouts when he sees me sit down across the table. I give him a savage little grin in reply.

The third attempt comes after the pie has been eaten and the coffee has been drunk and the youngest boys have wandered off. Weston is still sitting across from me, looking so bored and desperate. He touches *both* his ears (as if this will help influence me) and quirks his eyebrows.

Now?

I suppress a smile, slowly shaking my head.

Nope.

For someone whose middle name is "Stealth," he doesn't understand the concept of discretion very well. If we got up and left right now, everyone would question where we were going.

So I wait patiently for the perfect moment. And, sure enough, it arrives—when the adults decide to migrate into the living room and enjoy the rest of their coffee and conversation by the fireside. In the bustle of movement and empty plates being collected, I seize my opportunity.

"Dinner was absolutely delicious, Mrs. Ludovico," I say, reaching up to inconspicuously run my fingertip over my ear.

She smiles and says, "Oh, thank you, sweetheart."

"Thank *you*," I reply, fidgeting with my earring now. I bite down on a smirk, sliding my gaze to Weston—who is already staring at me intensely from across the table.

Now.

A spark lights up in his eyes, and he quickly stands, almost knocking his chair over. I trap a laugh in my fist.

He's so cute.

WESTON
DECEMBER 24

FINALLY.

I was starting to wonder if Tessa would ever let us sneak away, or if she was just having too much fun torturing me. Good thing she's so beautiful—she can get away with it.

To be honest, I'd be happy just staring at her in dumbstruck silence for the rest of the night. But I'm even happier when we escape together, whispering like spies in the hallway for a moment.

"I have to go get my gift for you," Tessa says. "It's in my bag."

I nod. "Mine's upstairs. I'll meet you in the den?"

"Sounds good."

We both smile and part ways—Tessa going back to the foyer and me heading upstairs to my room. That's when I remember that I didn't even wrap the stupid photo album.

It's too late now. Tessa will be waiting for me.

I curse under my breath, scanning my desk for something that would do the job—*anything*. On the floor, I find the square of vintage wrapping paper from the book that Tessa gave me on our date.

Perfect.

It's not too wrinkled from the first time it was used, and it's just the right size to cover the photo album. How's that for luck? It's a terrible wrapping job, but I don't care. Tessa is just going to rip it off in two minutes anyway.

Before I go back downstairs, I run into the bathroom to rinse my mouth and check my teeth—because I'm pretty sure that your-eyes-only gifts lead to making out (at least, I hope they do).

"Wes?" Noah's voice comes out of nowhere as I'm heading down the stairs. He pops his head out of his bedroom, where the sounds of Nintendo and Aidan's shouting can be heard. "What are you doing?"

"You didn't see me!" I say, and run from my little brother's curiosity like the plague. But no sooner am I downstairs than Henry ambushes me.

"What's going on?" he says, stopping me in the hallway.

I turn to face him—hiding Tessa's gift behind my back. "Nothing. Get back to Mom and Dad."

Henry crosses his arms over his chest. "That doesn't work on me anymore. Whatcha got there?" He dives behind me and snatches the album. "Oooh, I wonder who *this* is for—"

"Shh!" I grab the package out of his hand. "It's for Tessa, and I want everyone to just leave me alone for two minutes so I can give it to her."

Henry laughs. "I saw you guys leave together. Where is she? Your room?"

"No, she's in the den. And you'd better keep your mouth shut until we get back, or else."

Henry smirks. "That depends on how long you're gone. People might start asking *questions.*"

I point a threatening finger at him and say, "If you breathe a word about this, I will make sure you *never* get a dog."

"You're such a jerk..." Henry sighs and goes back to the living room.

If only he knew that he already has a dog and he owes Tessa one for taking care of it this whole time.

Finally, I make it to the den and find Tessa already there. She's sitting on the couch, waiting for me, her red dress glittering in the lamplight.

"Hi," she says with a little smile.

I swallow my pounding heart. "Hi."

"What took you so long? Did you lose it?"

"Lose what?"

"Your gift for me."

"Oh. Uh, no. No, it's... right here." I clear my throat awkwardly, shutting the door behind me and going over to sit next to her on the couch.

"It's not much," we both say at the exact same moment as we swap the gifts. Tessa bursts into giggles, her eyes sparkling.

God, I want to kiss her.

And not like I did under the mistletoe.

"You go first," Tessa says, gesturing towards the tiny package now in my hands. It feels like a book.

I shake my head. "No, you go first."

"No, you go first."

"No, *you* go first."

She rolls her eyes, heaving a sigh. "Fine." She starts to take off the wrapping paper (she's a peeler, not a ripper) and frowns curiously at it. "This paper looks familiar..."

"Does it?"

"Yeah, it's the one from the bookstore."

"Why do you always have to be so fricking observant?"

Tessa laughs. "What is it? Another book?"

I don't reply to that one, because the answer becomes obvious as the paper falls away. Tessa holds the photo album in her hands. The cover is pink cloth, with no title or picture or anything, so she doesn't actually know what it is until she opens the first page.

She drops the book in her lap and covers her mouth, tears springing to her eyes. "Oh my god," she gasps. "A photo album? For us?"

I smile, nodding.

The first picture is the one I always see on Tessa's lock screen: a selfie of us from a few months ago.

"This is one of my favorites," she whispers, tapping the photo with her sparkly red fingernail. "Oh my god, Weston... this is perfect." I watch as she flips through the rest of it, all the best photos we've taken together. Most of them are of her, photos she's never seen because I snap them all when she's not looking—like her petting the horses at Millbrook farm, looking cute as hell drinking a milkshake at the diner, playing with the golden retriever puppies, etcetera. Not to mention the countless selfies we've taken over the past few months.

"I love it," Tessa says, reaching the last picture. There are a lot of pages left, but they're all blank. "Did you not have time to finish it?" she asks, giving me a playful smirk.

"No," I reply, shaking my head. "We have all the time in the world to finish it."

Tessa smiles, her eyes lighting up as she understands what I mean. She leans in and surprises me with a fast, firm kiss. "That sounds wonderful," she whispers, squeezing my hand. "Thank you."

Mission accomplished.

But before I can kiss her to celebrate this success, she gulps in a shaky breath and says, "Okay, you open yours now because my heart won't stop racing until you do."

I almost forgot about the tiny package she put into my hand. "Oh. Okay."

I'm a paper-ripper. It's not reused from the bookstore, and it's all tied up with a ribbon and name tag that says "To: my sunshine," which makes me feel *really* lame for my half-assed wrapping job.

I pull the paper off, and it's…

"A notebook?" I observe brilliantly, turning it over in my hands.

Tessa rolls her eyes. "There's something *inside* it. Duh."

I grin because I love it when she makes that face. Then I open the notebook and find it already filled—with poems. Handwritten by Tessa.

I start to read the first one, and my heart slams the brakes.

If fate hadn't brought us together
I would do it myself

I'd go to the ends of the earth
to find you
to steal your heart
(thief that I am)
and give you my heart in return
and you'd say, "that's not mine."
and I'd say, "why don't you open it up and see?"
So you would look inside

(to prove me wrong)
but you wouldn't be able to
Because all you would find in my heart
is you.

They're all like this.

Love poem after love poem.

About me.

Holy crap.

It hits me in slow motion: Tessa didn't write these poems today. There are too many. She's been writing them for a while.

Probably weeks.

Probably months.

For a long moment, I'm speechless—all I can do is flip through the notebook, overwhelmed. If I believed in signs from God, I would definitely call this one of them.

After everything that's happened over the past few weeks—all the questions I never asked, the doubts I never let her know about, the gnawing sense of dread that kept me up at night... This book of poems is like the wrecking ball that smashes through it all and proves me wrong.

She loves me.

Like *this.*

Before I know it, all those buried emotions are rushing back at me like a tsunami, and suddenly there's a knot in my throat and tears in my eyes, blurring my vision.

Shit. I can't start crying in front of her...

But it's too late. Tessa sees and whispers, "Weston?" her voice hesitant and a little worried.

Of course she is. She has no idea what hell I've been putting myself through.

I swallow, closing the book and staring at it for a moment. I want to tell her so many things, but I don't think my voice will get very far. So instead, I just look her in the eyes and whisper, "Thank you."

She looks so surprised by my reaction, and I can tell she was totally not expecting me to start crying like a wuss—but I can't swallow it back any longer.

Tessa gives me a sad little smile as she takes my face in her hands. "I mean every last word in that book, Weston."

I nod—and one of my stupid tears falls right onto Tessa's hand. *Dammit.*

Her eyes are glossy, sparkling in the lamplight.

"I love you, Tessa," I rasp, my voice gone. My hands are trembling; my heart is pounding like a war drum in my chest.

I can't take it anymore.

I kiss her.

My hands blindly find her waist like a lifeline in the dark. I hold her gently as we kiss, as another stupid tear slides down my jaw. Her fingertips trace it—down my neck, over my chest, setting off fireworks inside me.

Wow.

My heart goes crazy as Tessa grabs a fistful of my shirt and pulls me closer. I feel her warm breath on my skin, her dress spilling into my lap as she moves closer.

I run my fingers through her hair; it feels like silk and smells like roses, and I can't get enough of it. Can't get enough of *her.*

Is this okay? I don't want to stop kissing her to ask.

I don't want to stop kissing her, ever.

Out of breath, we break away from each other. I laugh a little, feeling like such an amateur. But Tessa is gasping, too—still gripping a fistful of my shirt, her cheeks flushed and a few new strands of hair spilling into her face.

"We should probably go back," I whisper, "before someone comes looking for us."

Tessa nods slowly, relaxing her hold on me. "Yeah… yeah, you're probably right."

"I messed your hair up a little. Sorry…" I attempt to tuck the loose strands back in where they belong, but I can't make it look like it did before. A little sprig of baby's breath falls out of her hair and into my hand, but I don't put it back. Instead, I take it, kiss it, and press it inside the book of poems.

Tessa watches me do this, her big blue eyes so soft and beautiful it takes all my self-control not to start kissing her again—and mess her hair up even worse this time.

"You look… a little disheveled, too." She laughs under her breath, straightening my shirt collar. Her warm fingertips hesitate on my neck, and she gets this look in her eyes like she did when I made her ride that roller coaster forever ago and she loved it. Now I see that same adrenaline glittering in her eyes when she looks at *me*.

For a moment we just stare at each other like *holy shit what is happening* and finally we get so freaked out by this unexplainable electricity building between us that we both blurt out at the exact same time:

"We should go back."

I laugh. And she laughs.

And we go back.

197

Henry is the first to notice how "disheveled" Tessa and I look—I catch him laughing silently into his hands, and it makes me want to tackle him to the floor.

The parents notice, too. First Dad is like "There you two are," and then Tessa's mom says, "We almost sent out a search party to look for you!" and everyone starts laughing, and I'm blushing like hell, but Tessa is squeezing my hand so everything's okay.

Funny how you can hate your family and love them at the same time.

We hang out in the living room with them and talk for a while—Tessa and I sit on the floor by the fireplace, and I put my arm around her, and she holds my hand in her lap, and eventually she starts falling asleep with her head on my shoulder.

That's when her grandparents decide it's time for them to go home. I wish Tessa could stay. We could sleep on the floor together just like this and wake up on Christmas morning side by side.

Someday.

"I'll see you tomorrow morning," Tessa says softly to me before she leaves, "when I bring over the surprise for Henry."

I nod. "Sounds good."

Tessa grins, casting a glance at Henry, who is now asleep on the couch. "I can't wait to see his face."

"He'll be freaking out."

Tessa's grandmother calls to her—they're already halfway out the door. I grab Tessa's waist and pull her into one last kiss. "Thank you again… for the poems."

She smiles, her fingertip tracing my jaw. "Thank *you*."

"Goodnight, Tes."

"Goodnight, Wes."

As soon as Tessa leaves, I head up to my room. I lie on my bed, with a big idiotic smile on my face, as I read the book of poetry she gave me. It's almost like still having her with me. I can hear the words in her voice; the pages even smell like her. I lay the notebook open on my face and just breathe.

I wish you could see

what you look like

to me

Like colors I never knew existed

Like the first sign of spring after a long cold winter

Like the dawn after an endless night

Not just the silver lining,

but the light itself

I wish you could hear

what your voice sounds like

to me

Sunshine in the shape of words

a shout, a song, a whisper, a laugh

It's my favorite sound

no matter what

I wish you could feel

The wild thundering in my heart

when you kiss me

when I stop and think about how you're mine

it's like looking back at the earth from the surface of the moon

Wow.

TESSA
DECEMBER 25

I STILL WAKE UP AT FIVE A.M. ON CHRISTMAS MORNING.
It's the one childhood habit that I can't seem to break.

The first thing I do is reach for my phone and find a text from Weston glowing on my screen. It was sent three hours ago.

WESTON:

I've been up all night reading your poems and god
I love you so much. You looked so beautiful tonight
did I tell you that? if I forgot it was bc I was just
speechless. you're such an amazing writer and I'm
not just saying that bc the poems are about us. but
obvi that's the best part.) can I tell u something? idk
what my life was before you. it's like someone turned
on the lights and I'm just like damn I didn't know I was
living in the dark this whole time. like I thought things
were pretty good but then you showed up and made
my life 10000000000x more amazing and I seriously
don't know what I did to deserve it but I'm glad you

picked me ;) thank you.
oh hey look it's already Christmas lol... I hope this is
the first thing u see when u wake up.
Merry Christmas my love

I'm smiling the whole time I read Weston's message, a dizzying glow of happiness filling me up. It's unusual for him to send me an entire paragraph, let alone something so romantic and heartfelt. I screenshot the text for safekeeping and type him back a reply, although I'm sure he won't see it for hours if he really stayed up till two in the morning.

TESSA:
Good morning my sunshine <3
I hope this is the first thing YOU see when you
wake up: I love you more than I can say—those
poems are my best attempt to put into words how
I feel. but even they only scratch the surface. I don't
know what my life was before you, either. Maybe
we were just waiting for each other. Going down the
path of life and not knowing that our two paths would
intersect at just the right moment when we needed
each other most. thank you for picking ME. ;)
and Merry Christmas!!! get some sleep u silly boy

For a moment I close my eyes and remember the perfection of last night—the laughter, the tears, the way Weston kissed me when we were alone together. I never knew love could feel like this. It's like walking on air, like spacewalking through the vast, sparkling universe.

It's impossible to put into words.

I hope it never ends.

Springing out of bed, I pull on Weston's hoodie and go downstairs. It's still dark out, so I'm the only one awake—except for Thor, who is thrilled to see me. He spins around in circles, and I give him a good morning kiss, then slip on my boots and take him outside to go potty. When we're back inside, I give him his breakfast, which he vacuums down in a second, and then he stands there, wagging his tail and looking at me expectantly.

"Should we make cinnamon rolls?" I ask him, and he replies with a giddy little yip. I laugh. "Agreed."

Taking care to be as quiet as possible, I go into the kitchen and start making the dough. There's something so calming and cozy about baking while the rest of the world sleeps.

The whole house smells wonderful by the time Mom comes downstairs.

"You're up early," she says when I give her a hug.

"Yeah, I know. I can never sleep on Christmas morning."

The cinnamon rolls have just come out of the oven, so I make tea for both of us, and we sit at the kitchen table for a while, talking about last night. Mom asks me where Weston and I ran off to "all alone," and I blush as I tell her about our secret gift-swap. I show her the photo album that Weston gave me, and she agrees it's the sweetest present ever.

"How did he like the poems?" she asks.

"He loved them."

It seems like a feeble description of what really happened. But Weston was so vulnerable in that moment, tears in his eyes and his heart on his sleeve. I know I'm the only person he would cry in front of like that—and that makes our moment together more sacred and intimate. It's *our* moment. Only ours.

So I just give Mom a little smile and say again, "He loved them.

And then he kissed me, and, well… I got a little distracted by that."

She grins. "Mm, yeah, I could tell. You guys looked like you just got done playing seven minutes in heaven."

I laugh and blush even hotter, shaking my head. "It wasn't *that* risqué… Weston knows I have boundaries, and he respects them."

Mom nods. "Good. You're so much smarter than I was at your age."

"I don't know how smart I am. But I do see things more clearly now."

While waiting for Grandma and Grandpa to wake up, I show Mom a few cute apartments I found nearby—and thus, we get lost down the rabbit hole of Zillow, pointing out good prices and laughing at disastrous kitchen designs. It makes my heart feel so warm and light to plan for a future with Mom in it. To know that she's really, truly going to stay.

When Grandma and Grandpa come downstairs, Christmas morning really begins. We have coffee and cinnamon rolls in the living room while we open gifts. We always keep it minimal and casual, nothing too extravagant. It's more special that way.

My favorite gift is the music box Mom gives me. It's a hand-crank one, with a little window to look inside as the mechanism turns, plucking out the notes to the tune of "Rock-a-bye Baby." As soon as I recognize the song, I get all emotional; tears spring to my eyes.

I smile and kiss Mom's cheek. "I love it. Thank you."

Thor gets a present, too—a little red collar with a bone-shaped tag that reads *Thor*. "That's just part *one* of your gift, cutie." I laugh, snuggling him. "Ready to meet your new best friend?"

Mom and I drive over to Weston's house around nine o'clock, which we all agreed would be the best time to present the puppy. I have Mom stay in the car with Thor for a few minutes so that I can go inside and set up the surprise reveal.

"Merry Christmas, Tessa!" Noah shouts from the living room, where he's sitting on the floor, attempting to piece together an elaborate toy racetrack.

I smile, glancing around at the cheerful mess of Christmas morning aftermath. "Merry Christmas, Noah. Where's your brother?"

"Which one?"

I stifle a laugh. "Weston."

"Oh, um… he's somewhere. Him and Aidan are playing war."

I begin to hear thumping footsteps on the ceiling and Aidan's distant battle cries. I follow the sounds upstairs and quickly find myself in a Nerf war zone: the floors are littered with foam darts; barricades of empty Amazon boxes have been set up in the hallway. Aidan ducks behind one of the barricades, wielding a neon-orange Nerf gun and aggressively shooting at the doorway to Weston's room.

"Get out here and fight like a man!" he screams, then suddenly notices me standing at the top of the stairs. "Oh, hey, Tessa's here."

Weston laughs, still taking cover in his room. "If you think I'm gonna fall for that, bro, you've got another thing coming!"

I grin, crossing my arms over my chest.

That's when he leaps into the hallway with a belligerent roar, dual-wielding two Nerf guns. He doesn't see me standing there, and instead opens fire on his little brother, who dives behind the cardboard box barricade.

He couldn't look more different than he did last night. The posh prep school boy has been replaced by the Weston I'm more used to: a boy with messy hair, sweatpants and a *Star Wars* T-shirt. Somehow, he is just as attractive.

I stifle a laugh as I sneak up behind him. "Nice shot."

He startles and spins around to face me. "What the—Tessa?"

Aidan starts firing a giant yellow machine gun that spits foam balls faster than the others. Weston jumps in front of me so I don't get pelted with fake bullets.

"Hey, don't kill my girlfriend!" he roars at his little brother, but Aidan just laughs and keeps shooting like a maniac—hitting Weston right in the chest several times. Weston gasps dramatically, grabbing his chest as though he's really been shot. He throws himself on the floor, howling in pain. "Oh, OW! GOD SAVE ME!" He grabs my arm, pulling me down with him. "Kiss me before I die, Tessa."

I laugh, happily planting my lips on his while Aidan reloads his guns, laughing maniacally behind the Amazon boxes. Weston kisses me back, his hands in my hair for a moment—then he dramatically goes limp, playing dead.

I roll my eyes, leaning close to his ear and whispering, "I brought the dog."

His eyes fly open. "Yeah? Where is he?"

"In the car with my mom. She's waiting for your mom to smuggle him inside."

"This is like a spy mission," Weston mutters, crawling to his feet. "Cease fire, Aidan. I have to go find Mom."

"You can't just surrender!" Aidan yells, aiming his gun at his brother.

"I died! Okay? You win. Maybe I'll come back from the dead for another battle later." Weston grins, taking my hand as we head downstairs together.

Henry is in the living room, moping—though I can tell he's

trying to be grown-up about this disappointing Christmas. Weston and I act none the wiser as Mrs. Ludovico sneaks outside to get the dog.

Henry doesn't even look up when his mom comes back inside with Thor in her arms. Weston sees her and says, "So, no dog this Christmas, huh, bro?" He grins, messing up Henry's hair. "Better luck next year."

Henry glares at his brother, about to retort with something equally snarky, but that's when Mrs. Ludovico puts Thor down on the floor. He zooms over to Henry, yipping excitedly.

At first all he can do is stare at the puppy—his mouth hanging open in shock. We all start laughing, and his mom says, "Merry Christmas, sweetheart!" and that's when it sinks in.

"Oh my god!" Henry gasps as the puppy dives into his arms and starts happily licking his face. "For real? He's mine?"

"Well, he *does* have the perfect name," I point out.

Henry takes a closer look at the dog tag and laughs. "Thor! Holy crap, I can't believe this!" He hugs the puppy more fiercely, and the other boys, drawn to the living room by all the commotion, circle around to shower their new furry friend with affection.

I smile, my heart glowing as I watch the joyful scene unfold. Weston catches my eye, and he's smiling too. I'm pretty sure we just made this the best Christmas ever.

When Mrs. Ludovico starts explaining the whole story to Henry and the other boys, Weston grabs my hand and says, "Hey, I have one more gift for you."

I raise my eyebrows. "Really?"

"Yeah." He nods toward the door—and that's when I see he's holding his yellow ukulele. "Let's go out on the porch."

It's not too cold this morning, just chilly enough for a light flurry of snow to come swirling down on the world.

"Hey, look—Hollywood snow," Weston says, leading me over to the porch swing. "Perfect timing."

I grin, sitting down beside him. "For what?"

He doesn't tell me—instead he starts playing the ukulele. I watch his fingers move over the strings for a moment before I recognize the tune: "Auld Lang Syne."

A little excited scream leaps out of me, interrupting the music. I grab his face and kiss him, because I can't help it.

"Sorry, go ahead," I say with a laugh, sitting back. "I just love you."

He grins and says, "I love *you*, Tessa."

And he starts playing the song again, singing the lyrics this time. He has the loveliest voice, smooth and rich and soft. I fall more in love with him every time I hear it.

For the next verse, I join in—harmonizing with his voice. And there is nothing but the music between us, the snow swirling gently around us, and the magical glow of love in my heart.

THE END

❄ ❄ ❄

ACKNOWLEDGEMENTS

I can't quite believe I'm writing these words right now. I thought Tessa and Weston's story had come to a close at the end of *100 Days of Sunlight...* but it seems these beautiful characters had more to say. And you, my sweet reader, wanted to see more of them. So the story continued.

This book came to life amid a swirling cloud of holiday cheer and the tune of Bing Crosby's Christmas Classics. Many sugar cookies and cups of tea were consumed in the making of this little story, and I hope the joy in my heart has found its way through these pages and into your soul.

A huge thank you to my sister Kate, who read the messiest first draft and gave me the courage to keep writing. Thank you to my parents, two of the most inspiring people in the world. Thank you to my editing maestro, Jen, who always brings the magic finishing touch. And the biggest thank you to the WritersLife Wednesday community, who motivate me every single day to keep writing. This one is for you, my friends. Thank you for waiting so patiently and for being the most awesome support group. I love you all.

Rock on,
Abbie

ABOUT THE AUTHOR

ABBIE EMMONS has been writing stories ever since she could hold a pencil. What started out as an intrinsic love for storytelling has turned into her life-long passion. There's nothing Abbie likes better than writing (and reading) stories that are both heart-rending and humorous, with a touch of cute romance and a poignant streak of truth running through them.

Abbie is also a YouTuber, writing coach, filmmaker, big dreamer, and professional waffle-eater. When she's not writing or dreaming up new stories, you can find her with her nose in a book or binge-watching BBC Masterpiece dramas in her cozy Vermont home with a cup of tea. If you want to see Abbie in her element (ranting about stories) just type her name into YouTube and search.